M.C. Beaton (1936–2019) was the author of both the Agatha Raisin and Hamish Macbeth series, as well as numerous Regency romances. Her books have been translated into seventeen languages and have sold more than twenty-one million copies worldwide. She is consistently the most borrowed UK adult author in British libraries, and her Agatha Raisin books have been turned into a TV series on Sky.

The Hamish Macbeth series

DEATH
OF A CAD

M.C. Beaton

C

CONSTABLE

CONSTABLE

First published in the United States in 1987 by St Martin's
Press, 175 Fifth Avenue, New York, NY

First published in the UK in 2008 by Robinson,
an imprint of Constable & Robinson Ltd

This edition published in Great Britain in 2021 by Constable

1 3 5 7 9 10 8 6 4 2

Copyright © M. C. Beaton, 1987, 2008

The moral right of the author has been asserted.

A CIP catalogue record for this book
is available from the British Library.

ISBN: 978-1-4721-2407-4

Typeset in Palatino by Photoprint, Torquay
Printed and bound in Great Britain by Clays Ltd, Elcograf S.p.A.

Papers used by Constable are from well-managed forests
and other responsible sources

Constable
An imprint of
Little, Brown Book Group
Carmelite House
50 Victoria Embankment
London EC4Y 0DZ

An Hachette UK Company
www.hachette.co.uk

www.littlebrown.co.uk

Chapter One

Land of brown heath and shaggy wood,
Land of the mountain and the flood.
– Sir Walter Scott

Henry Withering, playwright, slumped down in the passenger seat of the estate car after another bleak look out at the forbidding landscape.

'Have we much farther to go, darling?' he asked plaintively.

'Oh, yes,' said his fiancée, Priscilla Halburton-Smythe, cheerfully. 'But we should be home before dark.'

Henry wondered whether to point out that, as they seemed to be surely approaching the land of the midnight sun after all those weary hours of travel, there was therefore very little hope of reaching their destination at all. He suddenly found himself too overpowered by the landscape and too depressed by the change it seemed to be creating in Priscilla to say anything, and so he decided to go to sleep

1

instead. But although he determinedly closed his eyes and listened to the hypnotic swish of the windscreen wipers, sleep would not come. Scotland had murdered sleep.

It was not that he, an Englishman born and bred, had never visited Scotland, it was just that he had never journeyed so far north before.

'It's clearing up,' came Priscilla's cool, amused voice. 'Do look. The scenery is magnificent.'

Henry reluctantly opened his eyes.

A watery sunlight was bathing the steep barren flanks of the towering mountains on either side. As the clouds rolled back, he found himself staring up at the awesome peaks and then around at the immediate prospect of damp sheep and bleak moorland.

The sun grew stronger and a wind arose. A river meandered beside the road, shining and glittering with red and gold lights. Then the scenery was blotted from view as they drove into a cutting. A waterfall hurtled down by the side of the road on Henry's side of the car, a relentless torrent that roared in his ear as they sped past.

He glanced out of the corner of his eyes at Priscilla. There was something rather frightening about a woman who could drive so well. They had left London at dawn, and she had driven the 640 miles north, sitting back, her hands resting easily on the wheel. She was wearing beige corduroy trousers and a cream silk blouse. Her fair hair was tied back behind her ears by a tightly rolled Hermès scarf. She looked sophisticated and elegant. But it seemed to him that there was a certain buoyancy in her manner as she neared her Scottish home, an excited anticipation that had nothing to do with him. In London, he had been used to a graceful and pliant Priscilla. After they were married, he decided, he would insist he did all the driving and that she should never wear trousers again. For the first time, he wondered if she would turn out in later years to be one of those terrible county ladies who managed everyone in the neighbourhood and opened fêtes. He sulkily closed his eyes. She was not even thinking of him, of that he was sure.

In this, he was wrong.

During the journey, a great deal of Priscilla's triumph at having secured a celebrity for a future husband had begun to ebb. She had told him to wear casual clothes, but he had turned up, impeccably dressed as usual, in white collar, striped shirt, old school tie, Savile Row suit, and shoes handmade by Lobb of St James's. She wondered uneasily what he had packed in his suitcase, whether he planned to startle the Highlands of Scotland by parading the countryside attired like a tailor's dummy.

When he had asked her to marry him, all she had felt was a giddy elation at having

3

done the right thing at last; at having finally found someone who would please her parents. Colonel and Mrs Halburton-Smythe had complained for a year because she had become a journalist, although Priscilla had tried, without success, to tell them that a job as a fashion editor's assistant hardly qualified her for the title. They had come on flying visits, always dragging some 'suitable' young man in tow. Priscilla realized uneasily she did not really know very much about Henry.

He was thirty-eight years of age, small, neat-featured, with smooth black hair and brown eyes that were almost black. His skin was sallow, and his legs were rather thin, but he had great charm and appeared to be universally popular.

Over the years, he had had various plays produced at experimental theatres, usually savage satires against the church and state. He was beloved by the Communists, Trotskyites, Marxists, and Liberals. To them, he was what they wanted most, a genuine ex-Eton schoolboy, son of a landed family who had opted to join the class war. He wore faded jeans and black sweaters and rather dirty sneakers.

And then his play *Duchess Darling* had opened in London. No one could understand what on earth had happened to Henry Withering. For it was a drawing room comedy of the type that opens with the butler and the cockney housemaid discussing their betters. It

4

had every cliché. Infidelity among the aristoc-racy, a silly-ass guardee, a gorgeous débutante, a stately duchess, and a bumbling duke. But the clothes were *haute couture* and it had a star-studded cast.

A clever impresario had decided that a London weary of inner-city riots, rape and politics might be in the mood for nostalgia. The left-wing papers stoutly gave it good reviews, convinced that Henry had written a very clever satire that they could not quite understand but were afraid to say so. The right-wing press were hesitant to damn it when the cast contained so many famous names who had been brought out of moth-balls. The public loved it. It was frivolous, silly, trite, and beautifully presented. They flocked in droves. After all, it was like going to a royal wedding. No one expected the stars to be clever, only to look very grand and rich. Henry's success was sealed when the left wing at last found out their darling had betrayed them and the Young Communists staged a protest outside the theatre during which five policemen were sent to hospital and a member of the Royal family was seen to frown. Henry's name appeared on the front page of every major newspaper the next day.

Priscilla's work as a fashion editor's assistant had mostly been arranging fashion photo-graphs, sitting around studios, shoving models in and out of fashions that were a cross between those of a medieval page and a Japanese labourer, and wondering whether the blue-rinsed lady she worked for was ever going to allow her a chance to write. She had finally been sent to write a report on the fashions in the play. She had gone backstage and had been introduced to Henry, who had promptly invited her out for dinner. One week later he had proposed. Now, one week after that, they were on the road to Priscilla's Scottish home at the express invitation of Priscilla's rapturously delighted parents, who were organizing a house party in honour of the new fiancé. Priscilla, at the age of twenty-three, was still a virgin. Henry had kissed her five times, and that had been the sum total of his love-making to date. She knew what he looked like in shorts because he had been photographed in tennis whites for a society magazine. But she had never seen him in person dressed other than as he was at that moment. It was odd that a man of his background should always look as if he were dressed for church, thought Priscilla, not knowing that Henry's clothes were a sort of costume to enhance his new darling-of-society image.

Beside her, Henry sat moodily listening to the rumbling of his stomach. They had stopped for a horrible lunch hours ago at a motorway café. He wanted his dinner. He wanted this nightmare journey to end.

Priscilla slowed to a stop and he looked up impatiently.

A shepherd was driving a flock of sheep down the centre of the road. He moved with an easy slow pace and did not look at the car. With an impatient grunt, Henry leaned across and honked the horn loudly. The sheep panicked and scattered.

'You awful fool,' snapped Priscilla. She rolled down the window. 'I'm very sorry, Mr Mackay,' she called. 'An accident.'

The shepherd came up and leaned in the car window. 'It's yerself, Miss Halburton-Smythe,' he said. 'Now, you should know better than to startle a man's sheep.'

'Sorry,' said Priscilla again. 'How's Mrs Mackay's leg?'

'Better, she says. We got a new doctor, Dr Brodie. He's given her the green bottle. She says it's awf'y good.'

'Are we going to sit here all day?' growled Henry.

The shepherd looked at him with mild surprise.

'My friend is tired,' said Priscilla. 'Must get on. Tell Mrs Mackay I shall call on her in a few days.'

'You mustn't hurry things in the country,' said Priscilla severely as they moved on. 'Mr Mackay was most offended.'

'Does it matter what the peasantry think?'

'They're not peasants,' said Priscilla. 'Really, Henry. I'm surprised at you.'

'Well, since you have promised to visit Mrs Mackay of the green bottle and the bad leg, I assume we must be nearly at our journey's end.'

'About another thirty miles to go.'

Henry groaned.

Lord and Lady Helmsdale sat in the back of their antique Rolls-Royce and shouted at each other, which was the way they normally conversed.

'If it weren't for this playwright-chappie, I would have turned down Mary's invitation,' said Lord Helmsdale. Mary was Mrs Halburton-Smythe.

Lord Helmsdale was small and round with thin grey hair combed carefully in strips over his bald patch. His wife was a huge woman, well over six feet tall, with a slab of a face. She was wearing an old tweed jacket and skirt and a shirt with a hard collar. On her head she sported an off-the-face blue-and-white-spotted hat. It looked remarkably like one Her Majesty had worn during her last American visit, and Lord Helmsdale had delayed their leaving by asking whether she had been ferreting around the rubbish bins at Buckingham Palace again. The resultant row had been frightful. But there is nothing more cosy than a shared marital resentment, and the Helmsdales were once more drawn together by their hatred of one of the Halburton-Smythe's guests.

The target of their hatred was Captain Peter Bartlett of the Highland Dragoons.

'Why on earth did Mary ask him?' demanded Lord Helmsdale querulously.

'If you mean Bartlett, then God knows,' snapped his wife. 'But I know *why* Bartlett's going to be there. He wants to bag the first brace.' She had long chats on the phone to Mrs Halburton-Smythe and never guessed for a moment how much that lady dreaded her calls.

'Didn't think there would be any grouse shooting,' observed his lordship. 'Grouse population's declining fast, and Halburton-Smythe told me not to bring my guns.'

The previous grouse season – which begins on August 12, known as the Glorious Twelfth, and ends on December 10 – had confirmed Scottish landowners' worst fears: The grouse were dying off fast, and that could soon mean an end to Scotland's £150 million-a-year grouse 'industry'.

'My birds are disappearing as well,' grumbled Lord Helmsdale. 'Think those Animal Rights people must be poisoning them to spite me.'

'Everyone's birds are dying off,' said his wife reasonably. 'The Game Conservancy has launched a three-hundred-thousand-pound appeal to finance research. They're appealing to all landowners for cash. Didn't you get their letter?'

'Can't remember,' said Lord Helmsdale.

'Sheikh Hamdan Al Maktoum has already given them a hundred thousand.'

'Mac who?'

'He's a United Arab Emirates Cabinet Minister who has a large estate in Scotland, and you ask me the same thing every time I mention his name.'

'Well, they won't need my money if they've got that much from him,' said her husband comfortably. 'Still, we needn't let Bartlett bother us. This playwright-chappie Withering's damned clever. Best play I've seen in ages.'

'I shall enjoy being rude to Bartlett,' remarked his wife. 'I shall enjoy that very much.

'The man's an utter cad.'

Jessica Villiers and Diana Bryce were best friends – the sort of odd friendship that springs up between a pretty girl and a plain one. Diana was secretly contemptuous of the mannish, gawky, horsy Jessica, and Jessica was bitterly jealous of Diana's stunning good looks.

Both girls' parents had estates over in Caithness in the north-east. Diana and Jessica had made their come-out at the London Season at the same time. Both worked in London and had taken their holidays at the same time, not out of friendship but because August was the fashionable time to holiday in Scotland.

The Highland grapevine works for the landed gentry in the same way as it does for everyone else there, and it seemed that no sooner had Mary Halburton-Smythe hit upon the idea of a small house party to welcome the playwright Henry Withering than she was besieged by pleading phone calls from all over. Everyone wanted to come, but she had kept the guest list down, and Jessica and Diana were two of that fortunate number. As Jessica competently managed her draughty old Land Rover along the single track Highland roads, Diana dreamt of snatching this famous playwright from under Priscilla's nose. Everyone knew Priscilla had about as much sex appeal as a fish. Diana had glossy black hair and a flawless complexion. The fact that the men hadn't exactly all fallen at her feet during her London Season still rankled. She had not yet learned the hard lesson that women who love themselves too much are rarely loved by anyone else. She had been engaged twice and on each occasion it had been the man who had called it off.

She would have been amazed had she known that Jessica was nourishing the same dream of wooing the playwright away from Priscilla. Jessica was convinced that the fellows, in the end, preferred a girl who was 'a good chap' rather than a posturing little miss . . . like Diana, she thought, casting a brief and evil look at her best friend. Of course, there had been that distressing business two years ago, she remembered, when Diana had become engaged to her, Jessica's, boyfriend. Of course, *that* engagement hadn't lasted – for how could any man enjoy the pleasures of Diana after having tasted those of Jessica?

'Who's going to be there?' asked Jessica. 'I mean apart from you and me and Priscilla and her fellow.'

'Oh, all the usual faces,' yawned Diana. 'By the time I had coerced Mrs Halburton-Smythe into inviting the both of us, I hadn't any energy left to ask who else was going to be there. There won't be any shooting with all this boring grouse problem, so I suppose the rest will be a lot of old fogies.'

Tommel Castle, home of the Halburton-Smythes, was not a real castle. It had been built by a beer baron in the nineteenth century, when Queen Victoria had made the Highlands fashionable by her visits: it had pinnacles, turrets, battlements, and a multitude of cold, dark rooms. The shallow oak stairs and corridors were guarded by fake suits of medieval armour.

Along the Highland roads heading for the castle sped the rest of the Halburton-Smythes' guests.

First to arrive was the raddled and still beautiful Mrs Vera Forbes-Grant and her banker husband, Freddy. They had a country home quite nearby. Then came Miss Prunella Smythe, a stage-struck spinster lady related to Colonel Halburton-Smythe who frequently wished she were not, and elderly Sir Humphrey Throgmorton, a collector of fine china who lived on the Scottish borders and was an old friend of the colonel.

Captain Peter Bartlett was already there, having arrived two days previously. As the first of the guests rolled up, he was lying fully dressed on his bed, admiring a silver cigarette box he had stolen from the library and wondering how much it would fetch.

Jeremy Pomfret had arrived in time for luncheon and was lolling in front of the library fire, tired from his drive up from Perth and too much food and wine.

He was a small, chubby man, and although he was nearly forty, he looked about twenty-five. He had a shock of whitish-fair hair and round blue eyes fringed with white lashes, which looked out ingenuously at the world from a cherubic face. He was very rich, and his passion was shooting anything at all that he was allowed to shoot.

He thought uneasily about the bet he had just made with Captain Peter Bartlett. Colonel Halburton-Smythe had told them at luncheon that he was not organizing a grouse shoot this year, on account of the mysterious dearth of the game birds. So the usual retinue of beaters, made up of crofters, itinerant farm labourers, and school-children on holiday, had not been hired. But anyone who wished to take his chances bagging a few brace on a walk-up was welcome to do so, the colonel had said.

Captain Bartlett had immediately turned to Jeremy.

'Brought your gun, laddie?' he asked, though everyone who was anyone knew that Jeremy Pomfret never went anywhere without a brace of shotguns.

'Yes, of course,' he replied.

'In that case, how about a bet to see which of us bags the first brace?'

And so the bet had been made, for five thousand pounds.

It had seemed perfectly reasonable and sportsmanlike at the time, especially to a mind mellowed with good claret. And five thousand pounds meant little to Jeremy. But now, sitting down by the fire and thinking it over, he began to have doubts.

Did Peter Bartlett actually have five thousand pounds to bet? He had met the captain before, briefly, at various social events in the Highlands and in London. He had always seemed a bit of a sponger, always broke. Why, then, was he so eager to bet what would be to him a large sum of money? What was Bartlett up to?

Anyway, the details were to be worked out the next night, when there was to be a buffet party held in this chap Henry Withering's honour, for Colonel Halburton-Smythe had suggested that the bet be made known to all the guests in case anyone wanted to make a side bet.

Still wondering what Bartlett could be up to, Jeremy Pomfret fell quietly asleep.

He snored gently through the noisy welcome being given to that famous playwright Henry Withering.

'This is where we turn off,' said Priscilla, slowing the car. 'We take this secondary road. The main road goes along the front of the village and stops outside the Lochdubh Hotel.'

For the first time that long and weary day, the scenery pleased Henry Withering's eye. 'Stop the car a minute,' he said. 'It's lovely.'

The village of Lochdubh lay on the shores of a sea loch of the same name. It consisted of a curve of eighteenth-century cottages, their white walls gleaming in the soft late-afternoon sun. A riot of pink and white Scottish roses tumbled over the garden fences. The waters of Lochdubh were calm and mirror-like. The air smelled of roses, salt water, seaweed, tar, and woodsmoke. A porpoise broke the glassy surface of the water, rolled lazily, and then disappeared. Henry drew a deep breath of pleasure as he watched the circle of ripples from the porpoise's dive widening and widening over the loch. A keening voice raised in a Gaelic lament arose from someone's radio.

'It makes London seem very far away – another country, a wrong world of bustle and noise and politics,' said Henry, half to himself.

Priscilla smiled at him, liking him again. She let in the clutch. 'We'll soon be home,' she said.

The car began to climb up a straight single track road away from the village. They reached the crest of the road and Henry twisted his head and looked back. The village nestled at the foot of two towering twisted mountains, their sides purple with heather. Then he realized they had stopped again. 'It's all right, darling,' he said. 'I'm too hungry to admire the scenery any longer.'

'It's not that. I just want to have a word with Hamish.'

Henry looked at her sharply. Her cheeks had a delicate tinge of pink. He looked ahead.

A tall, thin policeman was strolling down the road towards them. His peaked cap was pushed back on his head, and his fiery red hair glinted underneath it. He was in his shirt-sleeves, and the shine on his baggy uniform trousers above a large pair of ugly boots made it look as if he had ironed his trousers on the wrong side. He was carrying a bottle of Scotch under his arm.

What a great gangling idiot, thought Henry, amused.

But as the policeman recognized Priscilla and came up to the car, his thin face was lit up in a peculiarly sweet smile of welcome. His eyes were greenish-gold and framed with thick black lashes.

'It's yourself, Priscilla,' said the policeman in a soft, lilting accent.

Henry bristled like an angry dog. Who did this village bobby think he was, addressing Priscilla by her first name? Priscilla had rolled down the window. 'Henry,' she said, 'I would like to introduce Hamish Macbeth, our village policeman. Hamish, this is Henry Withering.'

'I heard you were coming,' said Hamish, bending down from his lanky height so that he could look in the car window on Priscilla's side. 'This place is in a fair uproar at the thought o' having a famous playwright among them.'

Henry gave a cool little smile. 'I am sure they are also excited to learn that Miss Halburton-Smythe is finally about to be married.'

One minute the policeman's face was at the car window, the next it had disappeared as he abruptly straightened up. Henry looked angrily at Priscilla, who was staring straight ahead.

Priscilla muttered something under her breath and opened the car door, nudging Hamish aside. Henry sat listening to their conversation.

'I did not know you were engaged,' he heard Hamish say softly.

'I thought you would have heard,' Priscilla whispered. 'You, of all people. You always hear the gossip first.'

'Aye, weel, I heard something to that effect, but I chust could not believe it,' said Hamish. 'Mrs Halburton-Smythe was aye saying you was to marry this one or that one.'

'Well, it's true this time.'

Henry angrily got out of the car. If he did not say something to stop this tête-à-tête, he had an awful feeling Priscilla was going to *apologize* to this village bobby for having become engaged.

'Evening, Officer,' he said, strolling around to join them.

'Why on earth are you carrying around that great bottle of whisky?' asked Priscilla.

'I won it at the clay-pigeon shooting over at Craig.' Hamish grinned.

'What an odd colour of Scotch,' said Priscilla. 'It's very pale, nearly white.'

'Weel, ye see,' said Hamish with a smile, 'the prizes was being giffen away by the laird, and his wife was alone in the tent wi' the prizes afore the presentation.'

'That explains it,' giggled Priscilla. She and Hamish smiled at each other, a smile that held a world of understanding and friendship from which Henry felt excluded.

'Explains what?' he demanded sharply.

'The laird's wife likes a drink,' said Priscilla. 'She drinks half what's in the prize bottles and then fills them up with water.'

She and Hamish burst out laughing.

'I am sure we are keeping you from your duties, Officer,' said Henry in what – he sincerely hoped – was his most patronizing tone of voice.

Hamish looked thoughtfully down at the playwright, his eyes, which a moment before had been full of laughter, suddenly blank and stupid.

'Aye, I've got to feed the hens,' he said. He touched his cap and turned away.

'Wait a minute, Hamish,' cried Priscilla, ignoring Henry's fulminating glare. 'Mummy's having a party tomorrow night in Henry's honour. Do come as well. It's drinks and buffet. Come at seven. Mummy doesn't like late affairs.'

'That's verra kind of you,' said Hamish.

'It's . . . it's black tie,' said Priscilla.

'I hae one o' those,' said Hamish equably.

'I mean dinner jacket and . . .'

'I'll find something.'

19

'See you then,' said Priscilla brightly.

Hamish loped off down the road. Priscilla turned slowly to face an outraged fiancé. 'Have you gone right out of your tiny mind?' demanded Henry.

'Hamish is an old friend,' said Priscilla, climbing back into the car.

Henry got in beside her and slammed the door shut with unnecessary force.

'Was that copper at any time anything more than an old friend?'

'Of course not, silly,' said Priscilla. 'You must remember, I know everyone in Lochdubh.'

'And are all the local yokels coming to this party?'

'No, Mummy's a bit of a snob and Daddy's worse and . . .'

Priscilla's voice trailed away.

She cringed inside as she thought of what her mother would say when she learned Hamish Macbeth had been invited.

Hamish – of all people!

Chapter Two

cad. Since 1900, a man devoid of fine instincts or delicate feelings.
– The Penguin Dictionary of Historical Slang

Jeremy Pomfret decided to have a bath before dinner. He shared a bathroom with Peter Bartlett and it was situated between their two bedrooms.

He threw off his clothes and wrapped his dressing gown around him. He pushed open the bathroom door and stood transfixed. Peter Bartlett was standing with one foot up on the washbasin, scrubbing his toenails. He was a very handsome man, dark and lean, with one of those saturnine faces portrayed on the covers of romances. He had a hard tanned face and a hard tanned body of which Jeremy was able to see quite a lot because the captain had only a small towel tied about his waist.

'I say,' bleated the horrified Jeremy. 'That's my toothbrush you're using.'

'Oh, is it?' said Peter indifferently. 'Give it a good rinse. It's not as if I've got AIDS.'

'Don't you realize the *enormity* of what you are doing?' demanded Jeremy in a voice squeaky with outrage. 'You're always pinching a chap's stuff. Yesterday it was my shaving brush. Now you're scrubbing your filthy toes with my toothbrush. Haven't you anything of your own?'

'It's all somewhere around,' said Peter vaguely. 'Met the playwright yet?'

'No, I fell asleep,' said Jeremy crossly, 'but I must say –'

'I know him.'

'How?'

'Met him in London before I rejoined the army. Awful little Commie he was then.'

'I'm sure it was just a pose,' said Jeremy, darting forward and snatching his toothbrush. He looked at it hopelessly and then threw it in the waste basket.

'In fact,' went on Peter, easing his foot down from the handbasin, 'this damned cold dump is crawling with skeletons out of my closet. The only person going to be at this party tomorrow night who I don't know is the village bobby.'

'What's he coming for? To guard the silver?'

'No, Priscilla asked him as an honoured guest. Henry told her parents about it before the rapturous welcomes were over, and

Halburton-Smythe hit the roof. He sent one of the maids down to the village with a note to the bobby to tell him not to come. Priscilla ups on her hind legs and calls him a snob, Mother joins in, and they were all at it hammer and tongs when I last saw them. But if I know Priscilla, she'll get her way in the end.'

'It's the first time I've ever stayed here,' said Jeremy. He was still smarting over the loss of his toothbrush, but he never had the courage to assert himself over anything. 'It'll be the last. I've never stayed anywhere quite so cold before. As soon as I bag my birds, I'll be off.'

'You might not win,' said Peter, leaning his broad shoulders against the bathroom wall.

Jeremy shrugged. 'Clear off, if you've finished, old man, and let me have a bath.'

'Righto,' said the captain, opening the door out of the bathroom that led to his room.

Jeremy sighed with relief and advanced on the bath. A grey ring marred its white porcelain sides.

'Dirty sod!' muttered Jeremy in a fury. 'Absolute dirty rotter. Complete and utter cad!'

Priscilla put down her hairbrush as she heard a knock at her bedroom door and went to answer it. Henry stood there, smiling apologetically.

'I am sorry, darling,' he said, taking her in his arms, and noticing again with irritation that she was several inches taller than he.

Priscilla extricated herself gently and went and sat down again at the dressing table. 'It was a bit thick,' she said. 'Did you have to tell them I'd invited Hamish as soon as we got in the door? I told you they wouldn't like it.'

'Yes, but you haven't yet told me *why* you were so bloody damned anxious to ask the bobby in the first place.'

'I like him, that's all,' said Priscilla crossly. 'He's a human being and that's more than you can say for most of the guests here. Jessica Villiers and Diana Bryce have never liked me. The Helmsdales are crashing bores. Jeremy's a twit. I don't know much about the gallant captain, but it reminds me of that rhyme about knowing two things about the horse, one of them is rather coarse. Prunella and Sir Humphrey are innocent sweeties but hardly strong enough to counteract the rest. Oh, let's not quarrel about Hamish. He's not coming and that's that. Don't dress for dinner. It's informal this evening.'

'Kiss me if you don't want to quarrel.'

Priscilla smiled and turned up her face. He kissed her warmly, and although she seemed rather to enjoy it, her reaction could hardly be called passionate. But it was not sexual desire that had prompted Henry to propose. Priscilla was, to him, all that a future bride should be.

He loved his new fame, he loved the money that came with it, and he loved his press image of being the darling of the upper set. The first moment he had set eyes on Priscilla, he had immediately seen her standing on the church steps beside him dressed in white satin and being photographed by every society magazine. She enhanced his image.

'Did you want to ask me something?' asked Priscilla when he had stopped kissing her.

'Yes, there doesn't seem to be a bath plug, and Mrs Halburton-Smythe told me not to ring for the servants because they don't have very many and the ones that she has might give notice if they had to run up and down the stairs too much.'

'Where is your room?'

'In the west turret, the one at the front.'

'Oh, *that* room. The plug in that bathroom was lost ages ago and we keep meaning to get another. But it's quite simple. It's a very small plug hole. You just stick your heel in it.'

'Not exactly gracious living.'

'No one really lives very graciously these days, unless you want masses of foreigners as servants, and Daddy is suspicious of anyone from south of Calais. I must say, you have rather grand ideas for an ex-member of the comrades.'

'I never was a member of the Communist Party.'

'But what about all those early plays of yours? All that class-war stuff.'

'It's the only way you can get a play put on these days,' said Henry with a tinge of bitterness. 'The big theatres only want trash. Only the small left-wing theatres will give the newcomer a chance. You've never said anything about *Duchess Darling*. Did you like it?'

'Yes,' said Priscilla. She had not liked it at all, thinking it silly and trite, but all her other friends had loved it, and Priscilla was so used to being at odds with them in matters of taste, she had begun to distrust her own judgement.

'I'll give you some of my better stuff to read when we get back to London,' he said eagerly.

He looked down at her with affection, enjoying the cool beauty of her blonde looks. When he received his knighthood, as he was sure he would, she would look regal in the press photographs.

He bent and kissed her again. 'I shall go and put my heel in the plug hole. I hope your mama has put us together at dinner.'

'Probably not,' said Priscilla. 'But we shall survive.'

Mrs Vera Forbes-Grant, clad only in pink French knickers and transparent bra, was sitting on the end of her bed, painting her toenails scarlet.

Her husband was sitting at the dressing table trying to add some more curl to his large handlebar moustache with his wife's electric hair curler.

'Your roots are showing,' he said, studying the top of his wife's bent head in the mirror.

'Well, they'll just need to show. I once went to the hairdresser here and the girls were so busy gossiping they nearly burned my scalp off. Seen Withering yet?'

'No,' said Freddy Forbes-Grant, 'but I've seen that rotter, Bartlett.'

'Damn!' Vera's hand shook suddenly, and the bottle of nail varnish tipped over on the carpet.

'Used to be pretty thick with him, didn't you?' pursued Freddy.

'Me? Course not. For God's sake, bring over that bottle of remover and help me clear up this mess.'

'Peter's here,' said Diana Bryce, flouncing into Jessica Villiers's room and banging the door behind her.

Jessica had been busy applying blusher to her cheeks. She stopped with the brush in mid-air. 'Awkward for you,' she said with an ugly laugh.

'Poor, poor Jessica,' said Diana sweetly. 'You will maintain that fiction that Peter ditched me. Everyone knows I ditched *him*.

But you were so crazy about him, poor lamb, you couldn't believe anyone would want rid of him.'

'Well, I ditched him before he got engaged to you on the rebound,' said Jessica breathlessly.

Diana eyed her with malicious amusement. 'Is that the case? I really must tease him about it.'

'And I must tease him about being given the push by you.'

Both girls glared at each other, and then Diana gave a little laugh. 'What nonsense we're talking. Who cares about him anyway? I thought we came to see the playwright.'

'Yes,' said Jessica slowly. 'I had almost forgotten.'

Henry Withering enjoyed dinner that evening immensely. He enjoyed the excellent food and the fake baronial dining room, hung with medieval banners that had been made in Birmingham twenty years before, when Colonel Halburton-Smythe had decided to redecorate the castle himself. He thought it was like a stage setting. The Halburton-Smythes did not run to footmen, but there were plenty of efficient Highland maids to serve the cold salmon *hors d'oeuvres*, followed by roast saddle of venison. There was a stately English butler to pour the wine. Lady Helmsdale, who was seated on Henry's right, did not once look at Captain Bartlett. Henry was rather sorry for Priscilla, who was at the other end of the table, with Lord Helmsdale on one side and old Sir Humphrey on the other. Henry had at first been wary of the good-looking captain, knowing of old his reputation with women, but in the drawing room before dinner, Priscilla had shown not the slightest flicker of interest in Peter Bartlett. Jessica and Diana had made a dead set at Henry, all very flattering and just as it should be. The fameless years of neglect were gone.

Henry was so busy being happily deafened by Lady Helmsdale's loud and fulsome compliments that he was unaware of any other conversation at the table.

Mrs Halburton-Smythe was a faded blonde woman with quick, timid movements. She was so often dominated by her husband that she rarely voiced an opinion on anything. She would even have allowed Priscilla to invite that dreadful joke of a policeman if her husband had not been so much against it. But it could be said in Mrs Halburton-Smythe's favour that she hardly ever listened to gossip, and that was why she had seated Captain Peter Bartlett between Jessica and Diana. Jessica tried to ignore the captain by talking to Jeremy, who was on her other side, while Diana picked at her food and stared sulkily in front of her, wondering what on earth Henry

29

Withering found so fascinating about the terrible Lady Helmsdale.

The captain, who had been drinking steadily, glanced to right and left and announced suddenly, 'Well, I must say you two girls make a lousy pair of po-faced dinner companions.'

Jessica shied like a horse and turned her head away. Diana affected not to hear. Opposite the captain, Mrs Vera Forbes-Grant leaned forward. 'I'll entertain you, darling,' she said in her husky whisky voice, 'if you don't think it rude to talk across the table.'

'I'm rather like you, old girl,' slurred the captain. 'Anything's permissible so long as it don't frighten the horses.'

'Oh, Peter.' Vera gave a nervous laugh. 'You're such a little boy when you try to shock. Do you think you'll get the first brace?' Word of the bet had already gone around the guests.

'Who knows?' said Peter. 'Damned birds have been dying off like flies. 'S all a Communist plot to ruin sport.'

'What on earth have the Reds got to do with a lot of game birds?' asked Vera.

'I'll tell you,' said the captain, leaning forward and putting his elbow in the remains of some cauliflower au gratin. 'Acid rain.'

'Acid rain?'

'Yes, they take it up frozen, see, in planes, above the moors, and they drop out great chunks of frozen acid rain on the grouse.'

'Oh, I see. They're *stunned* to death,' mocked Vera.

'Y'know, Vera,' said the captain, roaring to make himself heard above the boom of Lady Helmsdale's voice, 'you are one very dumb blonde . . . or would be if you got your roots done. Never seen them so black.'

'There's no need to get so bloody personal,' snapped Vera.

'What's the matter?' demanded her husband, Freddy, sharply.

'Peter's had too much to drink, that's all,' whispered Vera. 'Ignore him.'

But Peter Bartlett had found a new quarry. 'Turn the volume down a bit, Agatha,' he shouted suddenly in Lady Helmsdale's direction. 'Can't hear myself think.'

'You never can,' roared Lady Helmsdale. 'Don't you know it's because you never think?'

With one of his inexplicable changes of mood, the captain sent Lady Helmsdale an amused wink and then turned to Diana. 'You are looking very fetching tonight,' he said. 'I like that little black number. Suits you.'

Priscilla had met Peter Bartlett before but had never spent more than a few minutes in his company. She was amused to see how the obnoxious captain so easily turned on the charm. Diana was beginning to giggle and blush. Peter then said something across the table to Vera, who looked first startled, then gratified. Then he turned to Jessica and began to whisper in her ear until the frozen look of disapproval left her face and she began to look happy and excited. Priscilla then looked down the table to where Henry was laughing uproariously at something Lady Helmsdale had said.

He really is a pet, thought Priscilla. Mummy and Daddy are so pleased. It's nice to do the right thing for once. Poor Hamish. I do hope he won't feel the snub too painfully.

At that moment, Hamish was leaning on his garden gate outside the police station, enjoying the quiet evening. His slavering pet mongrel, Towser, as usual, had flopped down to sleep across his master's boots. Behind Hamish, from the back of the police station, came the mournful clucking of the hens.

The only thing that worried him was where to find a dinner jacket for the party. He had quickly recovered from the shock of Priscilla's engagement. Hamish had long ago discovered that it was easier to tuck painful things he could do nothing about at the present away into a far corner of his brain until such time as he could take some action.

He did not know the Halburton-Smythes had written to him not to come. Jessie, their dizzie housemaid, was walking out with Geordie, the baker's boy, and had met her swain only five yards from the police station. The encounter had made her forget the reason for her having been sent to the village. The housekeeper, Mrs Wilson, had told her to buy a packet of soap powder when she was down in the village, and Jessie remembered only that request. She did not find the note, undelivered, still in her apron pocket until two days later.

Chapter Three

Keep your place and silent be,
Game can hear and game can see.
                        – Mark Beaufoy

The members of the house party, with the
exception of the guest of honour, Henry
Withering, and his fiancée, Priscilla Halburton-
Smythe, looked rather jaded when they gathered in the dining room of the castle on the
following evening for the buffet supper.

Jeremy Pomfret appeared looking like a dissipated cherub, with blue circles under his
eyes. His room and Peter's had originally been
one triangular-shaped room. It had been con-
verted into two by a wall of thin plasterboard,
and the bathroom had been installed to cut
across the point of the triangle. Jeremy's sleep
had been disturbed by sounds of noisy
love-making coming from Peter's room all
night long. There had also been a lot of toing
and froing, and it had sounded as if the gallant

captain had been entertaining more than one lady during the night.

The beginnings of a very deep hatred for Peter Bartlett had begun to burn in Jeremy's old-fashioned, fastidious soul. That hatred had leaped into a flame that very evening, when Jeremy had gone into the bathroom to wash and shave before dinner. There were sopping-wet towels lying all over the floor, and there was a stomach-churning ring of hair round the bathtub, showing that Captain Peter Bartlett had shaved while he was having his bath.

'Filthy beast,' raged Jeremy, glowering at Peter across the room. The captain, lean, handsome, beautifully tailored, was being fawned on by Vera, Jessica, and Diana. How can any woman even tolerate being near the man? thought Jeremy. Tomorrow was the Glorious Twelfth, and Peter had still not yet said at what time he would be going out. It was not as if Jeremy could ask the servants; since it was only the pair of them, there were to be no loaders or beaters or even dogs.

Also looking the worse for wear were Lord and Lady Helmsdale. Both wore men's pyjamas in bed, and they had discovered last night that someone had poured glue into the crotch of each pair. They had spent hours trying to get the offending mess off the embarrassing places it had stuck to. They both blamed the captain.

Sir Humphrey Throgmorton sat listlessly in a corner. He never slept very well anyway. Prunella Smythe had stayed awake most of the night in a stagestruck fever of excitement. Freddy Forbes-Grant had been awakened by his wife's getting out of bed at two in the morning, saying she was going down to the kitchens to get a glass of milk. When she had not returned by three, he became anxious and went in search of her. When he had given up the search and returned to the bedroom, it was to find Vera once more in bed and fast asleep. He wondered what she had been up to, and that wonder had kept him awake and in a nasty temper until dawn.

Colonel and Mrs Halburton-Smythe had sat up very late debating whether their daughter actually meant to marry this splendid catch or whether she would change her mind. She had resisted their best efforts and had turned down so many eligibles that they found it hard to believe she meant to meet this one at the altar. They also planned to tell the captain to leave immediately after he had bagged his brace, but as they were both frightened of Peter Bartlett's erratic bouts of vicious temper, each wanted the other to give the captain his marching orders. They had never entertained him as a house guest before and had not realized until now the full horror of the captain's behaviour. They at last settled on that well-worn ruse employed by the landed gentry for speeding the unwelcome guest on his way – placing a railway timetable beside his bed with the soonest, fastest train underlined in red, and instructing the housekeeper to pack his case and leave it in the hall.

Whatever had put the shadows under the eyes of both Diana and Jessica, they were hugging to themselves, occasionally casting triumphant looks at each other, and then turning away puzzled, each obviously wondering what the other had to look triumphant about.

As well as the members of the house party, there was a sprinkling of local notables, now clustered about Henry, asking for his autograph and laughing at his slightest joke.

Priscilla was proud of Henry. He was so good-natured, so likeable, and so much at ease that all her doubts about their engagement had been laid to rest.

He had appeared during the day in respectably worn casual clothes and was now dressed in a beautifully tailored dinner jacket, the only relic of his past reputation for bohemianism being a pink-striped frilled shirt.

And then she looked across the dining room – it was the only large room in the castle, which was why it was being used for the party – and witnessed the full glory of the arrival of PC Macbeth.

Priscilla stifled a sharp exclamation of dismay and crossed the room to join him.

'Hamish,' she hissed, 'where on earth did you get that frightful dinner jacket from?'

'It's a wee bit on the short side,' admitted Hamish ruefully, looking down at his long, lanky figure. 'But wee Archie was the only waiter at the Lochdubh Hotel who was off duty tonight.'

The dinner jacket hung loosely on him and the sleeves only came three-quarters of the way down his arm, and his trousers were exposing a long length of woolly plaid sock.

'Come with me quickly,' urged Priscilla. 'Uncle Harry often leaves some of his gear here, and he's tall and thin. Mummy's glaring already.'

The Halburton-Smythes had double-barrelled their name after their marriage. Uncle Harry was Mr Paul Halburton, Mary Halburton-Smythe's brother, an archaeologist who travelled far and wide with the minimum of baggage and who always left most of his wardrobe behind at Tommel Castle after one of his flying visits.

Priscilla led Hamish quickly from the room before her mother could reach her.

Upstairs, in a cell-like room at the top of the castle, Priscilla rummaged through her Uncle Harry's wardrobe until she found a respectable dinner jacket and trousers. 'Put these on immediately, Hamish,' she said. 'You can hand them back tomorrow. I'll parcel up Archie's clothes and put the parcel in the hall and you can pick it up when you leave. Didn't you get my parents' message telling you not to come?'

'No,' said Hamish, removing the waiter's dinner jacket and then the abbreviated trousers. 'I would hae been most offended. I think, as it is, I should go home.'

Priscilla wrestled with her conscience. Her parents would be furious. But Hamish looked so miserable, and he did not seem to have much fun – except with some of the local ladies, Priscilla reminded herself sharply. But he saved every penny to send back to his mother and father and large brood of brothers and sisters over on the east and she was sure he never ate enough.

The door opened, and Jenkins, the Halburton-Smythe's English butler, walked in. Hamish was just about to put on Uncle Harry's trousers.

'Don't you ever knock?' snapped Priscilla.

'A good servant never knocks,' said Jenkins, his gooseberry eyes bulging with outrage. 'And what, may I ask, are you doing with this constable, and him without his trousers?'

'Don't be a silly twit, Jenkins,' said Priscilla. 'You saw Mr Macbeth arrive. He could not possibly put in an appearance in that awful dinner jacket, so I am lending him one of Uncle Harry's. What are you doing here anyway?'

'Mrs Halburton-Smythe sent me to look for

you. One of the maids said she had seen you coming up here.'

Priscilla bit her lip. Somehow it had never crossed her mind even to turn her back while Hamish was changing his trousers. She had become used to the fact that the Highlander, though quite prudish and shy in some respects, was never self-conscious about appearing undressed. But Jenkins was not a Highlander. And if she pleaded with Jenkins not to tell her mother what he had seen, that might make the whole innocent business seem sinister.

'Very well, Jenkins,' said Priscilla. 'You may go.'

'And what shall I tell Mrs Halburton-Smythe?' asked Jenkins, his eyes gleaming with malice. It was not that he disliked Priscilla in any way; it was just that he was a terrible snob and he thought Hamish Macbeth had no right to be attending Tommel Castle as one of the guests.

'Chust say,' said Hamish, whose Highland accent became more marked and sibilant when he was annoyed or upset, 'that Miss Halburton-Smythe will be doon the stairs shortly, and if you add anything to that statement, ye great pudding, I'll hear o' it and I'll take ye apart bit by bit.'

Jenkins glared awfully and then he wheeled about, his arms held out as if carrying a tray, and made a ponderous, stiff-legged exit.

41

'He's like a butler in a fillum,' said Hamish. 'I think when he feels his act or accent is slipping, he takes the bus down tae Strathbane and sees another old movie.'

'Don't blame old Jenkins too much,' said Priscilla ruefully. 'We must have looked like a bedroom farce.'

'How do I look now?' asked Hamish anxiously, straightening down the lapels of Uncle Harry's dinner jacket.

'Splendid,' said Priscilla, thinking privately what a difference good clothes made to Hamish's appearance. He was really quite a good-looking man with his red hair and clear hazel eyes, particularly when he was out of that joke of a uniform. It would be fun to take Hamish in hand. She gave herself a mental shake.

'Well, if you're ready, let's go,' she added.

'Are you sure it is all right?' asked Hamish, hesitating.

'You *shall* go to the ball,' said Priscilla with a grin.

Hamish moved closer to her and looked down at her shyly. 'You're looking awf'y pretty tonight, Priscilla.'

Priscilla always dressed in what pleased her and never bothered about the dictates of fashion. She was wearing a leaf-green chiffon blouse with a V-necked frilled collar and a black evening skirt. Her fair hair fell in a smooth line to her shoulders. Her only jewellery was the emerald-and-diamond engagement ring Henry had bought her at Aspreys. She looked up into Hamish's eyes and felt strangely awkward and uncomfortable. Up until that precise moment, Priscilla had always been at ease in the policeman's company. With Hamish, she felt obscurely that she could be herself and that Hamish would always like her no matter what she did. It was that old feeling of undemanding intimacy that had made her stay in the room while he changed his trousers. For the moment that easiness had fled, and Priscilla felt herself beginning to blush.

She took a step backwards and mumbled, 'Let's go.' Aware of Hamish's curious eyes on her, she scooped up the waiter's clothes, draped them over her arm, and hurried from the room without looking back to see if he was following her.

When she reached the dining room, she abandoned Hamish to his fate and went to join Henry. He was happily talking to his admirers and, to her relief, had not noticed her absence from the room.

At last she looked over to see how Hamish was faring. The policeman was engaged in conversation with Jeremy Pomfret and the Helmsdales. Priscilla's parents had been thwarted in their intention of throwing Hamish out by the Helmsdales' welcome of him. For Hamish took many prizes at shooting contests and Lord Helmsdale was one of his admirers, as was Jeremy Pomfret. Lady Helmsdale did not know Hamish, but she found him a nice, pleasant man with a refreshing air of shyness – unlike that horrible Peter Bartlett, that cad, who had now drunk enough to turn nasty.

Lady Helmsdale was further pleased when Hamish turned out to have intelligent views on the decline of the grouse population. 'If the decline continues,' said Hamish, 'most of Scotland's moor owners will hae no alternative but to opt for intensive sheep farming or forestry planting, and that would mean the loss of the heather and the heather accounts for ninety per cent of the grouse. It would also lead to a verra serious loss of sporting income, rural employment, not to mention the tourist revenue.'

Jeremy, encouraged by Hamish's shy, respectful manner, found courage to air his own views. Hamish listened with half an ear, while he picked up snippets of conversation from other parts of the room. While appearing to attend closely to Jeremy and the Helmsdales, he was indulging that intense Highland curiosity of his to the hilt.

There wasn't a woman as well-dressed as Priscilla in the room, he thought. Vera was wearing last year's fashion of slim sheath with three belts. But Vera was plump, and all she had achieved was three spare tyres instead of one. Hamish knew Vera by sight. He did not know Diana, but he thought it was a pity that such a beautiful girl should be dressed in funereal black that was bunched up, Japanese-style, about her middle. The horsy girl beside her, mused Hamish, turning his gaze on Jessica, should surely never have gone in for an orange strapless gown. Every time she moved her shoulders, her bones stuck out in all sorts of odd places.

Jessica and Diana had drawn a little aside from Vera and Peter.

'I wish you would stop staring at me in that smug way and saying how tired you are,' whispered Diana. 'If you've got one of the gamekeepers into your bed, you should keep quiet about it.'

'I would hardly call Peter a gamekeeper,' giggled Jessica.

'What!' Diana almost spluttered with rage. 'He was with *me*!'

'He couldn't have been,' said Jessica. 'He was with me.'

Both girls glared at each other and then gradually the anger died out of their eyes to be replaced by a look of mutual consternation.

'He couldn't be such a bastard. Even Peter couldn't do that,' whispered Diana. 'What time did he call on you?'

'Four in the morning,' said Jessica in a small voice. 'He didn't call on me. I went to him.'

'He told me to visit him at midnight,' said Diana miserably.

Both girls held hands like children and turned and looked at Peter Bartlett. His back was to them and Vera was facing him. They saw her full, pouting lips framing a kiss.

'And guess who was with him in-between-times,' said Jessica. Her eyes filled with tears. She took a step towards the captain.

'Don't,' said Diana. 'Don't let him know we've found him out. Let's get him for this. I could kill him.'

'I wouldn't flirt so blatantly if I were you,' Peter Bartlett was saying to Vera. 'Freddy might notice.'

Vera's eyes were soft. 'After last night, Peter darling,' she said, 'he can notice what he likes. We're made for each other.'

Peter never knew quite how it happened. A few drinks and he loved the world. A few more and his life seemed full of dead bores. He turned a jaundiced eye on Vera.

'I must say,' he said, 'you were certainly the best of last night's bunch. Lots to be said for middle-aged women with insatiable appetites.'

The smile slowly left Vera's face as the full implication of what he had said sank in.

'Who else was with you last night?' she demanded. 'Oh, darling, you must be joking. There can't have been anyone else.'

The captain's black eyes swivelled round to Jessica and Diana and then back to Vera. One eyelid drooped in a mocking wink.

Vera threw the contents of her glass in his face, burst into tears and ran from the room. Her husband saw her stumbling departure and ran after her.

Everyone began to talk very loudly as if nothing had happened.

Hamish had been studying the scene thoughtfully. He saw Priscilla waving to him and excused himself from the Helmsdales and Jeremy and went to join her.

'Henry's dying to speak to you again,' said Priscilla brightly. She had once more had to re-assure Henry that she had no interest whatso-ever in the village constable. Henry had finally noticed Hamish's presence in the room and had accused Priscilla of countermanding her parents' orders by re-inviting the constable herself. Priscilla had explained the reason for Hamish's presence, but Henry was still suspi-cious, although he covered his suspicions very well, and asked her to call Hamish over. He wanted to see the pair of them together again, just to put his mind at rest.

Right behind Hamish came the adoring Prunella Smythe. She was a middle-aged lady wearing a great many bits and pieces. Her hemline drooped. Bits of scarf and thin tatty necklaces hung around her neck. She had a scrappy stole around her thin shoulders with a moth-eaten fringe that had wound itself into the ends of her long dangling earrings.

Called by one and all 'Pruney', Miss Smythe's pale eyes behind her thick glasses looked out on the world with myopic wonder.

Before Henry could speak to Hamish, Pruney launched into full gush. 'I cannot tell you enough, Mr Withering, how much I adored your play.'

Peter Bartlett, who had been standing behind them mopping his face with a napkin, turned around. 'I never read anything but the *Racing Times*, Henry, but I did hear you'd got your smash hit at last. What's it about? The evil capitalists?'

'Oh, no,' said Pruney in a rush. 'Nothing like that *at all*. It's the most glorious drawing-room comedy, *quite* like the old days. None of those nasty swear words or –' her voice dropped to a stage whisper – '*sex*.'

'Sounds a bore,' said the captain.

Pruney giggled. 'It's actually quite naughty in bits. I love it when the duchess says, "Marital fidelity is so yawn-making."'

Henry turned as red as fire. 'Shut up!' he said rudely. 'I hate it when people quote my play. Shut up, do you hear!'

Pruney's short-sighted eyes filled with startled tears.

'Nasty Henry,' said Peter in high good humour. 'Come along, Miss Smythe. You shall tell me all about it. I could listen to you all night.'

He led the now gratified Pruney away.

'He can't even leave Pruney alone,' said Priscilla. 'That man's a menace.'

'He minds me o' Jimmy MacNeil down in the village,' said Hamish. 'That man would lay the cat.'

Priscilla rounded on Henry. 'What on earth came over you?' she asked. 'There was no need to rip up poor old Pruney like that.'

'How would you feel if you had spent years writing good solid plays and then only been accepted and famous after you'd deliberately produced a piece of twaddle,' said Henry in a hard flat voice. 'I can't even bear a line of *Duchess Darling*.'

'Oh, darling, I didn't know you had written it like that deliberately,' said Priscilla with warm sympathy. 'And I thought there was something up with me because I didn't like it. Never mind. After this success you can write what you like. Don't glower. Look! Food. I'm starving. Lead me to it.'

She slipped her arm through Henry's and led him away. Hamish watched them go. Priscilla gave Henry's arm a squeeze and then she bent and kissed his cheek.

Hamish trailed off to where Sir Humphrey Throgmorton was sitting alone. He introduced himself and asked Sir Humphrey if he could fetch him any food.

'Later, my boy. Later,' said Sir Humphrey. 'Sit down and talk for a bit. I'm too old to circulate and the sight of that bounder Bartlett makes me ill.'

'Quite a character,' said Hamish.

'He's rotten,' said old Sir Humphrey, his little grey beard waggling up and down. 'I could tell you a thing or two about that cad. The wonder is that he's never been in prison.'

Hamish looked down at him hopefully, waiting for more, but Sir Humphrey said, 'I *am* hungry after all. Could you please get me a plate of something?'

Over at the buffet, Hamish arranged a selection of cold meat and salad on a plate and took it back to Sir Humphrey.

Realizing he was hungry himself, he went back to the buffet. By the time he had picked out what he wanted, Sir Humphrey was happily talking to Lady Helmsdale. Then Hamish saw Diana waving to him. She was seated at a table in the corner with Jessica. The girls introduced themselves and Hamish merely said he was Hamish Macbeth, without adding that he was a policeman.

'Do you live near here?' asked Diana, her wide, almost purple eyes roaming over Uncle Harry's expensive suit.

'Down in the village,' said Hamish.

'Is your wife anywhere about?' asked Jessica.

'I am not married,' said Hamish.

Both girls brightened perceptibly.

'It's so nice to meet an unmarried man,' drawled Diana. 'These house parties can be a drag.'

'I'm not the only unmarried man here,' pointed out Hamish. 'I know Mr Pomfret is not married, and Mr Bartlett, I believe, is –'

'Forget about Peter,' said Jessica. 'No girl in her right mind would have anything to do with him. And Jeremy's a wet. Do eat your food . . . Hamish, is it?'

'Dangerous places, the Highlands, don't you think?' said Diana with a sly look at Jessica. 'All sorts of accidents can happen.'

'Like what?' asked Hamish.

'Oh, exposure, hypothermia, avalanches . . . things like that.'

'We had a murder here last year,' said Hamish.

'Yes, we all heard about that,' said Jessica. 'The murdered woman was a horrible character anyway. Don't you think it's mean when some poor person rids the earth of some obnoxious toad and then has to pay the penalty?'

'You can hardly expect me to agree with you,' said Hamish.

'Oh, why?'

'Not in my official bible,' said Hamish with a grin. 'Don't you know I'm the local bobby?'

'Oh, really?' said Diana, as if Hamish had just confessed to being the local cockroach.

'You're *that* Macbeth,' said Jessica in tones of loathing. 'I read about you in the papers.'

Hamish realized the air about him was becoming glacial and murmured something about taking his leave.

He stood up and looked about for Priscilla. She was sitting next to Henry and did not notice him. But Henry did, and put a possessive hand on Priscilla's knee.

He then thought he should grit his teeth and thank Mrs Halburton-Smythe for her hospitality, but as he approached her she gave him a horrified look and tried to hide behind a plant.

Hamish sighed and made his way to the door. Jeremy Pomfret seized his arm. 'I say,' he said, 'have you heard about this bet I've got on with Bartlett?'

'Aye, everyone's talking about it,' said Hamish. 'I hear there are a few side bets on, too.'

'Well, it's now been agreed that we go out at nine in the morning, each with a gun and cartridges, and go off in opposite directions. The first one back at the castle with a brace is the winner.'

'I wish you luck, Mr Pomfret,' said Hamish and turned to leave, but Jeremy clutched at his sleeve.

'I say, old chap,' he said urgently, 'couldn't you, well, sort of be around here at nine tomorrow morning, a sort of referee, you know?'

'What for, Mr Pomfret?'

Jeremy led Hamish into a corner.

'I don't trust the blighter,' he said in a hoarse whisper. 'You see, the bet's for five thousand pounds, and frankly, I don't believe he's got it. And he's been making some side bets, too. Unless I'm very much mistaken, that means he's certain he's going to win.'

'Maybe he's just full of confidence,' said Hamish cautiously. 'The captain's a verra good shot, I'm told. I'm sure you'll both get your brace tomorrow. The grouse may be a lot scarcer these days, but there are still plenty out there.'

'Yes, but without beaters or even a dog, it could take ages to walk up to a covey. Either of us could win. What worries me is why Bartlett is so certain it will be him, unless he's got some trick up his sleeve. Sure you won't come here at nine to see everything is above board?'

'I'd like to, Mr Pomfret,' said Hamish. 'But it's like this. Unless the colonel invites me, I chust cannot put my nose into this. And the colonel is not going to invite me. In fact, he sent word to stop me coming here tonight, but the message got lost on the way. Besides, any suggestion of a referee would mean the colonel would be made to look as if he thought one of his guests was about to cheat, and he wouldn't stand for that.'

'Yes, I see what you mean,' said Jeremy, pouting like a disappointed baby. 'Sorry to have troubled you.'

Hamish continued on his way out.

He picked up the parcel containing the waiter's clothes from a chair in the hall and made his way out on to the drive.

Peter Bartlett, smoking a cigar, was pacing up and down.

'Sobering up for the big day,' he said when he saw Hamish.

'Good luck,' said Hamish politely, fishing for his car keys.

'You've heard about the bet?' asked Bartlett.

Hamish nodded. 'I hear it's for quite a bit of money,' he said.

'Yes, quite a stroke of luck that, finding old Pomfret here.' Bartlett's white teeth gleamed in a broad smile. 'And I thought I was going to have to be content with that Arab's miserly two thousand pounds.'

Hamish, who had been about to open his car door, stopped and turned around. 'And what Arab would that be, Captain?' he asked slowly.

'Just some old oil sheikh in London. He's heard stories about the honour of dining on Scottish grouse on the day of the Glorious Twelfth itself, so I offered to get a brace for him – at a price, you understand.'

'And how will you get them to London in time for the sheikh's dinner, Captain?'

'He's paying for that. He'll have a helicopter here before nine in the morning. That'll take the birds to Inverness airport. The helicopter pilot will put them on the shuttle plane to London, and one of the sheikh's flunkeys will pick them up at London airport.'

Hamish studied the captain thoughtfully. 'And the sheikh will send you a cheque, I suppose?'

'Not likely. When I hand over the grouse, the helicopter pilot will hand me a packet – two thousand pounds in cash. I drive a hard bargain.'

'So,' said Hamish, 'if you bag a brace by noon or so, you're sure to get the two thousand?'

'Exactly,' said Peter Bartlett with a wolfish grin. 'Just can't lose.'

'So if you don't get the first brace, you'll only have to pay Mr Pomfret three thousand pounds. And, of course, those side bets you've been making.'

Peter Bartlett thrust his head forward, peering into Hamish's face in the gathering gloom. Then he threw back his head and laughed.

'Don't worry, my dear constable-chappie. I won't lose.'

'In that case,' said Hamish, opening his car door, 'I'll say goodnight.'

'Look here,' said the captain, putting a hand on Hamish's shoulder, 'do you believe in that thing, you know, where you can tell what's about to happen? The second sight – that's it.'

Hamish patiently turned around. He was accustomed to weeping drunks, fighting drunks, and psychic drunks.

'And just what do you think is going to happen?' he asked politely.

'I've got this feeling someone's out to get me,' said the captain. 'I feel a lot of menace about . . . oh, it's hard to explain.'

'I think it iss very easy to explain, Captain Bartlett,' said Hamish. 'If a man puts as many backs up as you have, then it iss almost a form of suicide. I haff met people before who could not bring themselves to put an end to their lives, and so they went around goading other people into doing it for them. Goodnight. Captain Bartlett.'

He drove off and left Peter Bartlett staring after him.

Chapter Four

I once read the last words of a suicide, in which he stated he hoped the jury would not return a verdict of 'accidental death' or 'death by misadventure', because he thoroughly understood what he was doing when he shot himself, and did not wish it handed down to posterity that he belonged to the class of idiots who inadvertently would handle a weapon in such a way as to cause risk to themselves or others.

– Charles Lancaster

Police Constable Hamish Macbeth did not sleep well. Towser lay at the end of his bed, across his feet, snoring dreadfully. The sleepless sea-gulls wheeled and screamed over the loch outside, an owl hooted mournfully, and then there came the sharp bark of a fox.

'And to think the tourists come here for the peace and quiet,' mumbled Hamish. After another futile hour of trying to fall asleep, he struggled out of bed. Although it was only five in the morning, the sky was already light. He looked out of his bedroom window, which faced over the loch.

It had been a bad summer to date, but this morning had all the signs of heralding a perfect day. A thin mist was rising from the glassy loch. The humped hills on the other side with their stands of larch and birch floated in the mist like a Chinese painting. He opened the window. The morning air was sweet with the smell of roses.

Hamish had succeeded in growing a splendid rambling rose over the door of the police station, and flowers rioted around the blue police sign and trailed over the steps.

The one cell in the police station had stood empty for a long time. The village drunk had joined Alcoholics Anonymous in Inverness and no more enlivened the little police station with nightly renderings of 'The Road to the Isles' and 'The Star o' Rabbie Burns'.

It was not a job for an ambitious man, but Hamish took his responsibilities seriously. He could make enough to send money home to his father and mother. His job meant he did not have to pay rent or pay for the use of the police car. It was the duty of every Celt to stay unmarried until the next in line was old enough to go out to work. But there had been a long gap between the birth of Hamish, now in his thirties, and the next Macbeth child, Murdo. And Murdo was proving to be a genius at school and would probably win a scholarship to university and so Hamish's responsibilities must go on a bit longer.

He decided to stay awake and scrambled into an old army sweater and his shiny regulation trousers. Uncle Harry's dinner jacket and trousers were hung carefully over a chair, the expensive cloth and tailoring looking out of place in Hamish's tiny shabby bedroom, like an aristocrat who has lost his way home from his club.

Towser rolled over on one side and spread himself comfortably out over the bed. Hamish looked down on the dog and sighed. There had been a time not so long ago when he had banished the dog from his bedroom – for what would, well, some girl think should she decide to share his bed?

But hope had gone. Now Hamish wondered gloomily if he was destined to share his bed with the mongrel for years to come.

He went out to the shed in the back garden to get the feed ready for the chickens and geese.

Henry had put his hand on Priscilla's knee. If only he could get that nasty little picture out of his mind.

He went about his morning chores and then went back inside and made himself a large breakfast, more for something to keep himself occupied than because he was hungry. Towser, smelling the frying bacon, slouched out of the bedroom, looking dazed and rumpled like a dissipated drunk, and placed a large yellowish paw on Hamish's knee, which was his lazy way of begging.

Hamish picked at his breakfast and then gave up and put his plate on the floor for Towser.

He decided to go down to the harbour and look at the catch brought in by the fishing boats.

As he walked along, he kept remembering snatches of overheard conversation from the party. That Vera had been insulted by Captain Bartlett had been all too evident. So was the fact that, up until a few moments before she had thrown her drink in his face, she had been madly in love with him. Perhaps Priscilla was better off with that neat little playwright of hers, thought Hamish gloomily. She might have become engaged to someone like Peter Bartlett. How old was Henry? wondered Hamish. Certainly a lot older than Priscilla. Even older than he was himself. Probably pushing forty. It would have somehow been more understandable if Priscilla had fallen for a man as young as herself.

Lochdubh was a sea loch. The little stone harbour smelled of fish and tar and salt. He was just debating whether to mooch some herring for his dinner when his sharp ears caught the sound of heavy snoring, rather like Towser's, coming from behind a pile of barrels stacked next to the sea-wall. He ambled around the barrels and stood looking down at the unlovely sight of Angus MacGregor, local layabout and poacher, lying on the ground between the barrels and the sea-wall. He smelled strongly of whisky. He was lying on his back, a shotgun cradled on his chest, and smiling beatifically.

Hamish bent down and gently removed the gun. Then he heaved the still-sleeping Angus over on his face and with experienced hands searched in the deep 'poacher's pocket' in the tail of Angus's coat. He lifted out a brace of dead grouse.

Angus had been warned off the Halburton-Smythe's estate many times. The last time a gamekeeper had given him a beating, but all that had done was to make Angus swear he would continue to take every bird and beast he felt like taking off the estate. When he was crazy with whisky, he often claimed to be Colonel Halburton-Smythe's bastard son. As Angus was about the same age as the colonel, no one even troubled to listen to the story – except Colonel Halburton-Smythe, who had been heard raging that one day he would shoot Angus and stop his lying mouth.

Hamish walked off with the brace dangling from his hand. He could not be bothered waking Angus up and charging him with theft. It was too fine a day. And taking a statement from Angus was always a wearisome business involving hours and hours of highly inventive Highland lies.

Then he remembered how Jeremy Pomfret had pressed him to 'referee' the contest for the first brace. Returning the grouse Angus had poached would give him an excuse to go to the castle and see what was happening. He might also see Priscilla.

Towser was panting for an outing when he returned to the police station, so he drove off with the large mongrel sitting up beside him on the passenger seat and the dead birds slung in the back.

The narrow road that led out of Lochdubh towards Tommel Castle wound through a chaos of tormented rocks, relics of the days when great glaciers had covered this part of the north-west of Scotland. In among the rocks, tarns filled high with water from the recent rains shone blue in the sun. These hundreds of tarns, or small pools, never failed to fascinate Hamish. On bright days, they scintillated sapphire-blue, and when the sky was heavy and grey mists twisted among the mountains, they glinted whitely or lay black and fathomless. The skies dictated the beauty of the scene, so that it was always changing, brilliant one day, weird and ghostly another.

Ahead reared up the fantastic pillared mountains of Sutherland, with quartzite sparkling on the upper slopes and the deep purple of heather on the foothills.

As he approached the castle, he caught a glimpse of red-and-white behind a stand of larch. He stopped the car and got out. A helicopter stood on a flat piece of ground behind the trees, the pilot leaning against its side, smoking a cigarette. Hamish looked at his watch. It was eight-thirty.

'Fancy anyone wanting to eat birds that hasnae been hung,' marvelled Hamish. 'Some of thae Arabs have more money than sense.'

A few minutes later, Hamish drove up to the front door of the castle. Jenkins, the butler, had observed his approach and was standing waiting inside the open door.

'The kitchen entrance is around the back,' he said.

'I ken that fine,' said Hamish. 'Aye, it's a grand day. I just want a wee word with Miss Halburton-Smythe.'

'That will not be possible,' said Jenkins stiffly. 'Miss Halburton-Smythe and the guests are at breakfast.'

Hamish looked over Jenkins's shoulder and the butler turned round.

Red-eyed and haggard, Jeremy Pomfret was marching up to them.

'That bastard Bartlett!' he shouted.

'I assume Captain Bartlett has gone out shooting,' said Jenkins.

'I thought so,' said Jeremy bitterly. 'He's not at breakfast and he's not in his room. And his gun's gone.' He noticed Hamish for the first time. 'You see, I told you he was up to something. Sneaked out early. Well, he's been found out and the bet's off. Came to my room last night with a bottle of champers. "Have a drink, old boy," says he. Made me drink the whole bottle. Said we'd meet up at breakfast and go out together, and all the time the bastard was planning to get up early an' beat me to it. God, I feel awful.'

'Aye, it's a terrible thing when they force the stuff down your throat,' said Hamish amiably.

'He didn't force it,' muttered Jeremy. 'But when a chap offers another chap champagne, a chap can't refuse.'

'True, true,' said Hamish, leaning lazily against the castle door. 'It's awf'y hard to say no to the champagne.'

'I have already told you, Mr Macbeth,' said Jenkins, 'that Miss Halburton-Smythe is not to be disturbed.'

Hamish recognized one of the maids who was crossing the hall with a tray. 'Jessie,' he said, 'be a good girl and tell Miss Halburton-Smythe I want a wee word with her.'

'Sure thing,' said Jessie, who was an American movie addict.

'Jessie,' said Jenkins sharply. 'I have informed this constable that Miss Halburton-Smythe is at breakfast.'

But Jessie either didn't hear, or pretended not to hear. Jenkins clucked with irritation and went after her.

'What are you going to do now?' asked Hamish, turning his attention back to Jeremy.

'Nothing, not with this hangover. I've a mouth on me like a Turkish wrestler's jock strap. I'm going back to bed.'

He trailed wearily back up the stairs.

Priscilla came out of the dining room into the hall. She was wearing biscuit-coloured linen trousers, thin sandals, and a frilly Laura Ashley blouse. Her blonde hair was pinned up on top of her head. She looked as fresh as the morning.

'What did you want to see me about?' she asked Hamish.

Hamish, who had been staring at her, pulled himself together. 'I wondered if you would like me to bring over Uncle Harry's clothes or whether you would like to collect them from the police station.'

Priscilla looked amused. 'Instead of coming all the way up here to ask me what to do,' she said, 'you could have brought the clothes along with you and solved the problem.'

'Och, so I could've,' said Hamish stupidly. 'There's another thing. Angus, the poacher, was down by the harbour and –'

He broke off and cocked his head to one side. Someone was running hard up the gravel of the drive.

He went out to the front steps, with Priscilla after him.

John Sinclair, the estate's head gamekeeper, came running towards them. 'He's shot hisself,' he cried. 'Oh, what a mess!'

'Who is it?' demanded Priscilla, pushing in front of Hamish.

'It's Captain Bartlett, and he's got a great hole blown clean through him.'

Priscilla turned and clutched at Hamish's sweater in a dazed way. Sinclair ran on into the castle, shouting the news.

'It's awful,' whispered Priscilla, beginning to shake. 'Oh, Hamish, we'd better go and look. He might still be alive.'

He put his arms around her and held her close. 'No, I don't think so,' he said in a flat voice.

The guests, headed by Colonel Halburton-Smythe, came tumbling out of the castle. Henry Withering stopped short at the sight of Priscilla enfolded in Hamish's arms.

'Lead the way, Sinclair,' barked the colonel. 'And you, Jenkins, call the ambulance. The ladies had better stay behind. Macbeth, what are you doing here? Oh, never mind, you'd better come with me.'

Hamish released Priscilla and set out with the colonel and the gamekeeper. Henry, Freddy Forbes-Grant, and Lord Helmsdale followed. Sir Humphrey Throgmorton returned to the castle with the ladies.

The day was becoming hot. The air was

66

heavy with the thrum of insects and the honey-laden smell of the heather.

As they left the castle gardens, Colonel Halburton-Smythe spotted the helicopter. 'What the hell is that thing doing on my property?' he demanded. Hamish explained about the Arabs in London and the promised payoff of £2,000.

'Bartlett had no right to order helicopters to descend on my land without asking me,' said the colonel. 'Oh, well, the man's dead and he won't be needing that two thousand now.'

'Aye, that's right,' said Hamish, looking thoughtfully at the helicopter.

'Don't stand there as if you'd never seen a helicopter before,' said Colonel Halburton-Smythe impatiently.

Hamish fell into step with the others and they set out over the moors at a steady pace.

It should have been raining, thought Hamish, steady, weeping rain like they had had during the previous weeks. A tragedy in bright sunshine seemed much more frightful than one on a day when the skies were grey.

'Here we are,' said the gamekeeper, pointing ahead.

The ground sloped down. At the bottom of the slope was a wire fence. Hanging over the fence was a body, still and grotesque and unreal in the clear air.

'What a mess!' whispered Lord Helmsdale in awe as they reached the scene.

Captain Bartlett hung almost upside-down, suspended by his right leg from the top strand of the fence. The gun was on the other side of the fence, its butt in a gorse bush, the side-by-side barrels resting on the top strand of the fence, glaring wickedly like two black fathomless eyes at the group. There was no doubt the captain had been straddling the fence when he was shot.

'Don't touch anything,' said Hamish. 'The forensic boys from Strathbane will need to see everything.'

They stood around Hamish in white-faced silence.

The sun was hot. A buzzard sailed high in the clear air.

Then Lord Helmsdale cleared his throat noisily. 'You can see what happened, Macbeth,' he said, his voice once more loud and robust. 'The silly ass was using his gun as a support to balance himself as he climbed over. Everyone does it. Do it myself. Then the gun got caught in that damned bush, and when he tried to pull it clear, the triggers snagged and went off. Must have been both barrels. Look! He's blown a hole clear through his chest.'

There were violent retching noises as Freddy threw up in the heather.

'But how could that happen?' asked Henry in a shaky voice. 'There are two triggers, and besides, wouldn't he have the safety catch on?'

'He should have,' said Hamish. He stepped around the body and peered at the gun. 'But the safety catch is off. Verra careless, that. Now, those thorns are tough and springy and if the front trigger got caught, and if the captain pulled hard enough, it could pull both triggers.'

Hamish walked a few yards away and stepped easily over the fence so as not to disturb the body. He circled the gorse bush. 'It is an accident that sometimes happens,' he said. 'Even experienced sportsmen close a gun and then forget it is loaded.'

Hamish took out a clean handkerchief, took hold of the gun by the barrels, and slowly and carefully extricated it from the bush.

The gun was a Purdey, a hammerless sidelock, self-opening ejector gun. Hamish whistled softly. 'A pair o' these would set ye back around thirty-five thousand pounds,' he said.

He broke open the gun and took out two cartridges. Both were spent. He glanced at the body. 'Both barrels.' He held up the spent cartridges. 'Number six,' he said, half to himself. He laid the gun down carefully on the heather and knelt down by the fence. Carefully, he reached through the wires and felt inside the captain's jacket pockets. The others watched, fascinated, as the policeman withdrew a handful of unused cartridges. He examined them and nodded. 'Number six as well,' he said. He then stood for a long time in silence, staring at the dead man. The captain's tweed cap had fallen from his head and lay in the heather. He had been wearing a shooting jacket, corduroy knee breeches, wool socks, and thick-soled shoes when he had been shot.

Henry said sharply, 'The man's shot himself by accident. I don't see any need for the rest of us to hang about. How you can stand there, Macbeth, staring at that awful wreck of a man as if you were looking at a piece of meat on a butcher's block, beats me. And what were you doing,' he added his voice suddenly shrill, 'hugging Priscilla?'

'Policeman never did know his place,' said Colonel Halburton-Smythe.

'She was shocked and in need of comfort,' said Hamish, his eyes still fixed on the body. 'Perhaps, Mr Withering, it would be as well if you went back and looked after her. There's nothing anyone can do until the forensic team arrives from Strathbane. Would you call Strathbane police and get them to send up a forensic team as well as an ambulance?' he asked the colonel. 'I'd better stay with the body until they get here.'

'Better get Freddy away quick,' said Lord Helmsdale. 'Looks as if he's going to faint.'

'I'll be along shortly to get statements from everyone,' said Hamish.

'Why?' demanded the colonel. 'It's obviously an accident.'

'Oh, just in case,' said Hamish vaguely.

'Well, I have no doubt the matter will be taken out of your incompetent hands,' said the colonel viciously, 'as soon as the detectives from Strathbane arrive with the forensic team.'

'Just so,' said Hamish absentmindedly.

The rest began to trail away. Henry looked back. Hamish was still standing looking down at the body.

'I think that copper's off his head,' he grumbled.

'He's cunning and lazy,' said Colonel Halburton-Smythe. 'And devoid of natural feeling. He'll probably lie down and go to sleep when we're out of sight.'

'Known Priscilla long, has he?' asked Henry.

'Priscilla knows everyone in the village,' said the colonel. 'She is too easygoing and good-natured. Macbeth takes advantage of her kindness. Priscilla doesn't know quite when to draw the line. She even went off to a film show in the village hall with Macbeth last year. I had to warn him off. Thank goodness she's marrying you, Henry.'

'Would you like me to wait with Macbeth?' asked Sinclair, the gamekeeper.

'No,' said the colonel. 'I want you to be on hand to answer questions when the police arrive from Strathbane.'

When they were out of sight, Hamish climbed back over the fence to the side where the captain was half-hanging, half-lying. He

71

opened the captain's game bag, which was slung around his neck, and peered inside. It was empty. He reached up to push his cap back on his head and then realized he had not put on the rest of his uniform, bar his trousers. He wished he had brought Towser with him instead of leaving the animal cooped up in the car.

He bent down and searched the springy heather near the dead man. Then, crawling along on all fours, he began to search away from the body. 'It's chust too convenient – that's what gets me,' he muttered. 'He was coming away from the moor and without his brace. Had he given up? But there's grouse available. Angus got his brace easily enough.' He thought back to the party. No one had seemed to like the captain. The three women who had been clustered around him when he, Hamish, had arrived had turned cold and angry and bitter. And who was that girl who had suddenly begun to talk about accidents?

He searched while the sun climbed higher in the sky and its rays beat down on his head.

Then he heard the sound of voices and looked up. Walking over the crest of the hill came a familiar heavy-set figure, sweating in a double-breasted suit.

Hamish recognized Detective Chief Inspector Blair with his sidekicks, detectives Jimmy Anderson and Harry MacNab.

After them came ambulance stretcher-bearers and the forensic team and three uni-formed policemen.

Hamish knew the investigation was about to be taken out of his hands. Although he had once solved a case and let Blair take the credit, he knew that Blair had now convinced himself that he, Hamish, had had nothing to do with it.

Walking back to stand beside the dead body, Hamish bent down and looked in the game bag again. Something caught his eye. As Blair marched up to him, Hamish slid one small grouse feather into the pocket of his trousers.

Chapter Five

. . . nothing in his life became him
like the leaving of it. . . .
                    – Shakespeare

Detective Chief Inspector Blair was not a Highlander. He had been brought up in Glasgow, that city which produces some of the brightest brains in the world, along with some of the biggest chips on the shoulder. Blair, as Hamish often remarked, had a chip on his shoulder so big, it was a wonder his arm didn't fall off.

Blair detested the upper classes because they made him feel inferior, and the Highlanders because they lacked any inferiority complex whatsoever.

But as he stood in front of the fireplace in the drawing room of Tommel Castle late that afternoon, he was enjoying himself. The Halburton-Smythes and their guests were grouped around him. On either side of Blair stood detectives Anderson and MacNab – like a couple of wally dugs, thought Hamish, who was standing by the window, meaning like those pairs of china dogs that not so long ago ornamented many mantelpieces in Scotland and have now become collector's items.

Strained faces, white in the gloom of the drawing room, which had been built facing north so that the sun should not fade the carpet, turned towards Blair.

'It was a straightforward accident,' he said. Someone let out a sharp sigh of relief. There was a palpable air of slackening tension in the room.

'So,' went on Blair, enjoying their relief and glad he had kept these toffee-nosed creeps waiting so long for his verdict, 'there'll be no need for me to take any more statements from you.' He had been unable to interview the helicopter pilot, for while he was examining the scene of the crime, Hamish had returned to the helicopter, taken the pilot's statement, and had told him he could return to Inverness, a piece of high-handedness that had driven Blair wild with rage.

He cast a venomous look in Hamish's direction before going on with his lecture.

'It appears that Captain Bartlett went out very early so as to cheat on his bet and have first chance at thae birdies.' Jeremy Pomfret winced. 'But before he could use his gun to shoot them, he used it to help himself get over the wire fence. The gorse bush caught the double trigger, and boom, boom, goodbye world.'

'For heaven's sake, man, show a bit of respect for the dead,' snapped Colonel Halburton-Smythe.

Blair rounded on him. 'You should be grateful tae me for finding out so quickly it was an accident instead of suspecting you all of murder.'

'Any fool could see it was an accident,' boomed Lady Helmsdale.

'Anyway,' went on Blair in a loud, hectoring voice, 'his gun was loaded with number six shot. It went off and blew a hole through his chest. The pathologist has already confirmed that the shot found in the remains of his chest was number six. The colonel of his regiment has been informed of his death. As far as the colonel knows, Bartlett had no close relatives still alive. He'll be sending someone over this week to pick up the captain's effects just in case a relative turns up.'

'He had an aunt in London, I think,' said Diana, and then turned pink.

'Anyway,' said Blair, 'the procedure is this. In cases of fatal accident, the procurator fiscal studies the pathologist's report and the police reports. Then an inquiry is held – in camera, so you won't have to worry about the press. It may be in a week's time or a month's time, so remember, even if you've gone back home, you must be ready to go to Strathbane when you're summoned.'

The door of the drawing room opened and Jenkins came in, followed by two maids carrying tea, cakes and scones.

Blair licked his lips and looked longingly at the teapot.

'Thank you, Mr Blair,' said Mrs Halburton-Smythe. 'If you have nothing further to add, I see no reason for you to stay.'

Blair flushed angrily. The least they could have done was to have offered him a cup of tea. He wanted to vent his anger on someone and looked about for Hamish Macbeth. But the Highland constable appeared to have vanished.

Blair crammed on his soft felt hat and signalled to Anderson and MacNab and strutted from the room.

Hamish had not left. He had had no lunch and wanted to see if he could manage to get some tea and scones. He had slid quietly down behind a large sofa by the window and was sitting on a small footstool.

Jessie, the maid, had a soft spot for Hamish. She quietly handed him down a plate of scones and a cup of tea when Jenkins wasn't looking.

Hamish drank his tea and listened to the conversation.

'Poor Peter,' came Vera's choked voice. 'What an awful death.'

'As if you cared,' said Jessica, suddenly and loudly. 'It's a good thing it wasn't murder, considering we all saw you throwing a glass of gin over him.'

'You leave my wife alone, young lady,' said Freddy. 'Captain Bartlett was a rotter and a cad, and I'm not going to pretend he was otherwise just because he's dead.'

'I thought he ... he was rather nice,' ventured Pruney Smythe timidly.

'Oh, he could charm anything in skirts and he didn't give a damn about age or appearance,' said Jessica with a nasty laugh. She had meant to hurt Vera, but the shaft struck home in Pruney's spinster bosom and she burst into tears.

'Now look what you've done, you horrible thing, you,' said Priscilla. 'Come with me, Pruney. You'll feel better after you've had a lie-down.'

Mrs Halburton-Smythe raised her voice. It held a note of steel. Afternoon tea in the drawing room was the one social event over which she was allowed complete control without interference from her domineering and fussy husband. 'These remarks are all in bad form,' she said. 'The man is dead and the least we can do is show some respect. We have all had a harrowing day, a lot of it unnecessarily harrowing. That man Blair is an uncouth pig. Hamish Macbeth may be a useless scrounger, but at least he's not abrasive. Now, the crofters' fair is to be held in Lochdubh in five days' time and the Mod wants us to help raise funds. And, Henry dear, it quite slipped my mind. The Crofters Commission has asked me if you will be good enough to present the prizes.'

'I'd love to,' said Henry, looking gratified. 'What on earth is the Mod?'

'It's a Gaelic festival of song,' said Priscilla, coming back into the room. 'We usually run the White Elephant stand. The crofters' sale is good fun and you can pick up some great bargains in hand-knitted woollies and thingies made out of deer horn. Oh, and the sheepskin rugs they sell are very cheap.'

Jenkins came in, looking hot and annoyed. 'It is the gentlemen of the press,' he said. 'They are all outside the front door talking to that man Blair.'

'Then clear them off the estate,' snapped the colonel. 'If that idiot Macbeth would only do his job. Phone him at the police station, Jenkins, and tell him to come here immediately. Once Blair starts pontificating to the press, he'll be here all night.'

Hamish felt himself going hot with embarrassment and wished he had not stayed to scrounge tea. He knew Jessie would not betray him, but if anyone in the room walked over to the window, they would find him.

He slid on to the floor and rolled his thin, lanky body under the sofa.

The voices rose and fell, becoming more animated as the shadow of sudden death rolled away. Jenkins came back to say that there was no reply from the police station, only a rude recording of a voice singing in Gaelic. Hamish groaned to himself. He never checked his answering machine, for the simple reason that since he had had a second-hand one installed two months ago, he had forgotten to play it back. The previous owner had obviously used the tape for recording his favorite Gaelic tunes.

Hamish shared the Highlander's weakness for second-hand gadgets and machinery of all kinds and, like his peers, was apt promptly to lose interest in the new toy immediately after he had got it.

The guests began to leave to spend the time before dinner in their rooms.

Hamish was about to crawl out from under the sofa and make his escape when a weight on his side told him that two people had sat down on it.

'It's been a violent introduction to the Highlands, I'm afraid,' came Priscilla's voice.

'Poor Peter,' replied Henry Withering. 'I'd hate to pop off and then sit up there hearing everyone down here being so glad I'd gone. Don't worry, Priscilla darling. I think I'm getting to like this place, despite all the dramatics. Would you like to live up here once we're married?'

'I never thought of it,' said Priscilla. 'I always assumed you'd want to be in London. But if you think you can bear being somewhere so remote ... well, I would love to live here. Not in the castle, I mean. Somewhere of our own.'

'We'll build our own castle,' said Henry. 'Come here. I've been longing to kiss you all day.'

Hamish sweated with embarrassment.

Henry put his arm about Priscilla's shoulders. She felt suddenly shy and looked down. Her gaze sharpened. A long bony hand crept out from under the sofa and tapped her foot. She stifled a scream.

'What's the matter?' demanded Henry.

But Priscilla had recognized that edge of navy sweater above the hand. 'I'm still shaky,' she said with a laugh. 'Come and walk with me in the garden. I've got to get some fresh air. It's stifling in here.'

Hamish waited until the sound of their voices had died away. Then he rolled out from under the sofa, opened the drawing room window, and climbed out. He made his way cautiously round the castle to the front without meeting anyone. The press had gone. His car was hidden behind the vast bulk of the Helmsdales' antique Rolls-Royce. Towser gave him a sad, reproachful look.

'Aye, it's like an oven in here,' said Hamish.

'I'll just take you home and give you a drink of water.'

The sunlight was now soft and golden as Hamish drove along the waterfront. Fishing boats were lined up at the pier, bobbing gently in a slow oily swell that was rolling in from the Atlantic. I hope it disnae rain, thought Hamish. I still have things to look for.

When he had fed and watered Towser and turned the dog loose in the garden, he poked around his small kitchen looking for something to eat. There was nothing in his refrigerator but an old piece of haggis and some black pudding. He opened the food cupboard and found a can of beans. Then he went out to the hen-house and collected five eggs.

He was settling down to a dinner of fried egg and beans and strong tea when he heard Towser yipping an ecstatic welcome.

'Come in,' he shouted, 'the door's open.'

Thinking it would be one of the villagers, he got to his feet to look for another cup.

'And what were you doing, hiding under the sofa, Hamish?' said a cool, amused voice.

Hamish put the heavy pottery cup he had just lifted out back in the cupboard and brought down a delicate china cup and saucer instead.

'It's yourself, Priscilla,' he said. 'Sit down and have a cup of tea.'

'Is that your dinner?' asked Priscilla.

Hamish looked thoughtfully at his half-eaten eggs and beans.

'Well, to my way of thinking, it is more like the high tea,' he said eventually. 'I would not be distinguishing it with the title of dinner. Do you want some?'

'No, I have to get home soon. Dinner is at eight and I've got to change. But I'll have a cup of tea. Now, Hamish . . .'

'I was searching for clues,' said Hamish, looking at her hopefully.

Priscilla slowly shook her head. 'The truth, Hamish.'

Hamish gave a sigh. 'I was that thirsty and I wanted some tea. Jessie saw me sitting down behind the sofa and gave me some when no one was looking. Then I felt guilty and I thought your father would have a fit if he saw me, so I slid under the sofa. I couldnae bear the idea of you courting and me listening,' said Hamish, blushing and averting his eyes, 'so I had to attract your attention.'

'You are the most terrible scrounger I have ever met,' giggled Priscilla. 'Still, it can't have been nice for you having to deal with Blair again. What a brute of a man! Thank goodness it was an accident. Can you imagine if someone had bumped off the terrible captain what it would be like? All our faces splashed over the tabloids.'

Hamish buried his nose in his cup. 'Does

it no' surprise you,' he said at last, 'that it wasn't a murder?'

'Not really,' said Priscilla, after a pause. 'The world's full of hateful people, but no one bumps them off. Too often the people murdered are innocent kids going home from school or old-age pensioners. Things are getting worse in the south, you know. Sutherland must be the last place on God's earth where you don't have to lock your door at night.'

'I wouldn't be too sure o' that,' said Hamish. 'I'm troubled in my mind. I keep seeing him with his chest shot to hell, hanging over that wire fence like a bunch o' rags. I knew of him afore this – the wild Captain Bartlett. Never to speak to, mind. I mean, I knew him by sight. He was full of life and not so bad when he hadn't the drink taken. The fence wasn't all that high. He had long legs on him. The way I see it, he would normally have pushed the wire down and stepped over.'

'It's an accident that's happened before, even to good marksmen, Hamish.'

'Aye, maybe.'

'You're not eating your food.'

'I hate baked beans,' said Hamish, loudly and forcibly. What he really meant was that he hated Priscilla's being engaged to Henry Withering, and felt he must vent his feelings somehow.

'Oh, wait a minute. I'll be back soon,' said Priscilla, exasperated.

She returned five minutes later carrying a small parcel. 'I knocked at the back door of the butcher's. Mr MacPherson was still there and I got you two lamb chops. Go and get some potatoes out of the garden and I'll fix you dinner.'

Soon Hamish was sitting down to a meal of grilled lamb chops, fried potatoes, and lettuce from the garden.

'It's very kind of you, Priscilla,' he said. 'I don't want to keep you. I thought you would be wanting to run back to Henry.'

'I'll see him at dinner,' said Priscilla vaguely.

Priscilla was filled with a sudden reluctance to leave the narrow, cluttered kitchen at the back of the police station. The back door was open, and homely smells of wood-smoke, kippers, and strong tea drifted in as the villagers of Lochdubh settled down for the evening. It was six-thirty, but very few people, apart from the Halburton-Smythes, ate as late as eight in the evening.

Henry had kissed her very passionately and said he would join her in her bed that night. At the time, Priscilla had said nothing to put him off, feeling it ridiculous in this modern day and age to hang on to a virginity she was soon to lose anyway. But Hamish emitted an aura of an old-fashioned world of courting, walking home in the evening, and holding hands; a world where it was all right to remain a virgin until your wedding night.

What would it be like, mused Priscilla, to be a policeman's wife? Perhaps the sheer boredom of living in a tiny remote place like Lochdubh would make her nervous and restless. And yet she had said she would live there with Henry.

'I had better go home,' she said, collecting her handbag.

'Aye,' said Hamish sadly.

They stood looking at each other for a long moment and then Priscilla gave an odd, jerky nod of her head and turned and left.

Hamish sat for a long time staring into space. Then he got out the car, called Towser, and drove off in the direction of the Halburton-Smythes' estate. He had driven halfway there when he saw the poacher, Angus MacGregor, walking along. He was not carrying his gun and had the dazed look of a man who has been asleep all day long.

Stopping the car, Hamish called him over. 'I should book you, Angus,' he said.

'Whit fur?' demanded the poacher, his bloodshot eyes raised to the sky as if calling on heaven to witness this persecution at the hands of the law.

'I found you dead-drunk down at the harbour this morning,' said Hamish, 'and in your back pocket was a brace o' grouse. You'd been poaching on the Halburton-Smythes' estate again, ye daft auld fool.'

'Me!' screeched Angus, beating his breast.

He began to rock to and fro, keening in Gaelic, 'Ochone, ochone.'

'Shut up and listen to me. I'll not be taking you down to the police station. I hae something in mind for you,' said Hamish, staring ahead, drumming his long fingers on the steering wheel.

Then he said, 'I want to see you the morn's morn with that dog o' yours, Angus. I've a bit o' work for you.'

'And what iss a man to get paid?'

'A man gets nothing. A man does not get his fat head punched. Be at the police station at six, or I'll come looking for you.'

Hamish drove off. He drew to a halt again where he had seen the helicopter and got out with Towser at his heels.

He walked until he had reached the scene of the captain's death and then he said to Towser, 'Fetch!'

Towser was an indiscriminate fetcher. He brought everything he could find if asked. Hamish sat down on a clump of heather to wait.

He looked up at the sky. Little feathery clouds, gold and tinged with pink, spread a broad band of beauty over the westering sun. The colour of the heather deepened to dark purple. The fantastic mountains stood out sharply against the sky. As every Highlander knows, the ghosts and fairies come out at dusk. The huge boulders scattered over the moorland took on weird, dark, hunched shapes, like an army of trolls on the march.

Hamish lay back in the heather, his hands behind his head, as Towser fetched and fetched. At last he sat up.

There was a small stack of items at his feet. Five old rusty tin cans, a sock, an old boot, one of those cheap digital watches people throw away when the battery runs out, the charred remains of a travelling blanket, an old thermos, and a broken piece of fishing rod.

Towser emerged, panting through the heather, dragging a piece of old tyre.

'Enough, boy,' said Hamish. 'We'll be back tomorrow. Maybe we're searching too near.'

'Not tonight, Henry,' said Priscilla Halburton-Smythe. 'It's this terrible death. I think I'm feeling shocked. I simply don't feel romantic. I'm awfully sorry.'

'All right,' said Henry sulkily. 'If that's the way you feel ... Where did you vanish to early this evening?'

'Just out. I felt I had to get out. Goodnight, darling. I'll be back to normal tomorrow.'

She gently closed her bedroom door in his face.

Jenkins marched into the breakfast room in the morning and stood to attention before his master. 'Sinclair has just been to report that

Hamish Macbeth, that poacher MacGregor, and their dogs are out on our moors, sir.'

'The devil they are,' said the colonel, turning red. 'Didn't he tell them to hop it?'

'Sinclair did, sir, but Macbeth said he was within his rights. He said he was looking for clues.'

'The insolence of that man is beyond anything,' said the colonel. 'Phone Strathbane and tell Blair to come over here and give Macbeth the dressing down of his life, and if he doesn't get over here sharpish, I shall report him to his superiors.'

'Certainly, sir,' said Jenkins with a satisfied smile.

The guests looked at each other uneasily.

'What is he doing?' asked Diana. 'I mean, it was an accident.'

'He's probably poaching,' said Colonel Halburton-Smythe. 'I know that man poaches. He's only using this looking-for-clues nonsense to cover up the fact he's a poacher himself. And what is he doing with that rascal MacGregor, if he's not poaching?'

Jenkins came back into the room. 'Strathbane says that Mr Blair is already on his way here. He wanted to assure you personally that the procurator fiscal's report tallied with his own. In fact, he should be here now.'

'Good,' said the colonel. There was the sound of an arriving car scrunching on the gravel outside. 'That'll be him,' said the colonel. 'Show him in.'

Blair could easily have phoned in the news, but he was still smarting over what he considered the Halburton-Smythes' rudeness in not offering him tea and, like most thin-skinned people who have been snubbed, he could not leave the snubbers alone.

His fury on learning that Hamish was supposedly looking for clues was tinged with satisfaction. He was in a vile temper and giving Hamish a bawling out appealed to him immensely.

'I'll go out and see him now,' said Blair.

Priscilla looked up and saw Hamish, with Angus MacGregor behind him, standing at the entrance to the breakfast room. She signalled wildly to him to escape, but Hamish stayed where he was, his face unusually set and grim.

'Good morning, Chief Inspector,' said Hamish.

Blair swung about, his piggy eyes gleaming. He opened his mouth to yell.

'It was murder,' said Hamish Macbeth. 'Captain Peter Bartlett was murdered. And I hae the proof o' it right here.'

Blair's mouth dropped open and he stared stupidly. A heavy shocked silence fell on the room.

Into that silence came again the soft Highland voice of PC Macbeth.

'Och, aye,' he said. 'It was nearly the perfect murder.'

Chapter Six

You may kill or you may miss,
But at all times think of this –
'All the pheasants ever bred
Won't repay for one man dead.'
                    – Mark Beaufoy

Hamish walked into the room and placed a red-and-white plastic shopping bag on a small table by the window. He rummaged in the bag, then turned around, holding up to the stunned gathering two spent shotgun cartridges.

'These,' he said, 'are number seven shot, not number six.'

There was a puzzled silence, finally broken by Blair. 'What the devil are you talking about, you great gowk?' he cried furiously. 'What has all this nonsense got to do with murder?'

'I think these belonged to Captain Bartlett, and I think he used them yesterday,' said Hamish, unperturbed.

'Nonsense,' said Blair. 'Anyone could have fired them.'

'But the captain was the only one out shooting,' replied Hamish, inwardly sending an apology up to heaven for the lie when he thought of Angus the poacher's brace of grouse. But Angus had just assured him they had been shot miles from where the captain died, although still on the estate, and Hamish had years of experience of knowing when the poacher was telling the truth and when he was lying. 'Besides, the season just began yesterday.'

'Then they were from last season,' said Blair with a pitying smile.

'Och, no,' said Hamish. 'The last season's shooting ended in December, eight months ago. They haven't been lying out on the moor all that time, in all that rain and snow.'

Lord Helmsdale nodded in agreement. Blair saw that nod and felt his lovely neat accident verdict beginning to slip away. 'Get on with it, then,' he snarled.

Hamish turned back to the plastic bag and produced two grouse. He held them up.

'I found these hidden in the heather, not very far from where the captain was murdered. Angus's dog found them. I think we shall find that they were killed with number seven shot, with these –' he held up the two spent cartridges – 'and that the captain had bagged them before he was killed.'

'Oh, aye?' sneered Blair. 'Your poacher friend found them, did he? Maybe that was because *he* bagged them and *he* hid them away.'

'Well, he was up on the moor on the morning of the murder,' admitted Hamish.

'And what number of shot does *he* use?'

'Number six,' said Hamish.

'Bartlett was shot with number six, so, if it was murder, then, you great pillock, your friend did it!'

'Och, but he couldn't have ...' Hamish began, but Blair started to interrupt. He was silenced by Lord Helmsdale.

'Let Macbeth speak,' said Lord Helmsdale crossly. 'When it comes to guns and shooting, he knows what he's talking about.'

Blair looked about to protest, but then he nodded to Hamish to continue.

'The time of the shooting was put at around seven in the morning,' said Hamish. 'I was down at the harbour at seven and there was Angus, sleeping like a pig. So he didn't murder the captain.'

There was a restless stirring among the small audience. I didn't know Hamish could look so cold and hard, thought Priscilla illogically. She glanced round at the others. All were staring fixedly at Blair, as if willing the detective to prove Hamish wrong.

'How did you come to this ridiculous conclusion?' scoffed Colonel Halburton-Smythe.

'Murder, indeed! Those grouse and cartridges don't mean a thing.'

'Well,' said Hamish, 'you remember when we found the captain, he had been climbing over the fence when he was shot.'

'Yes, yes,' said the colonel testily.

Hamish glanced quickly at the others who had come with them to the scene of the shooting – Henry, Freddy and Lord Helmsdale. They all nodded.

'Good,' said Hamish. 'We're all agreed. Now, it is obvious Bartlett was coming in this direction, away from the moor. So, that could only mean, as his game bag was empty and his gun still loaded, that he had been unable to bag his brace and was giving up and heading back here. He should have unloaded the gun, but people are careless sometimes, and that's how they shoot themselves accidentally.'

'Just like Bartlett did,' said Blair, looking triumphantly around the room, but Hamish continued as if he had not heard him.

'But I stepped easily over that fence, and the captain's legs are – were – as long as mine, so there was no need for him to use the gun to help himself over. That's what made me suspicious in the first place.

'So I checked the game bag again and it wasn't empty.' There was a sharp intake of breath from someone in the room. Hamish turned and dipped again into the plastic bag. From it, he produced a small box for carrying fishing hooks. He took something out and held it up. They craned forward to see. It was a tiny feather, a greyish feather with a brown tip. 'A breast feather from a grouse,' said Hamish. 'And there was another one.' He held it up. 'It was lying on the ground near the body.

'It looked to me as if the captain *had* bagged his brace before he died. So that would mean he was on his way back here. And it would also mean he would not have needed to reload the gun. It meant, too, that someone had removed the grouse from the bag, and that someone –' he looked slowly round the room – 'is the one who murdered him.'

'Look, laddie,' said Blair heavily, 'say Bartlett was going to cheat and get his grouse before the agreed time, then why wouldn't he have been the one who hid them in the heather, ready to be picked up quickly and get them first to the castle to win the bet, and then to the helicopter to ship them to London?' Everyone knew by this time what the helicopter had been doing there.

Hamish's soft voice went inexorably on. 'The captain was too experienced on the moors. He would know there would be a great likelihood of a fox picking them up. And if not, the crows would have found them. There was already a crow picking at this pair when we got to them. They wouldn't have been in any fit state to go to London.'

'This is all very well,' said Diana in a strained voice. 'But I don't quite understand what you're getting at. How did the murderer go about it?'

'This is how I think it happened,' said Hamish. 'I believe that the murderer intended to kill the captain sometime during their stay here. If the captain had gone out at nine o'clock as agreed, he couldn't have managed it, what with people up and awake. He would have waited for another opportunity.

'But the captain decided to cheat and left at dawn. The murderer must have seen him, realized what he was up to, and saw his opportunity to kill him without a witness. He followed him out to the moor, taking a gun and cartridges with him.

'It wouldn't have been easy to find him in the poor light, but when the captain got his brace, the murderer followed the sound of the shots. He met the captain on his way back here to the castle and they came face-to-face as the captain stepped over that fence.

'The murderer fired both barrels at point-blank range. What he did next shows he is a very clever man indeed. He opened the captain's gun and found it unloaded. He checked the game bag and found the grouse, so he knew the gun had been fired. He took the spent cartridges from his own gun, the ones that had killed the captain, and put them in the captain's gun, closed it again, then carefully tangled it in the gorse bush. Now it looked like an accident.

'But our murderer was more than just clever. He examined the captain's pockets and came across a handful of unused cartridges. They were number seven shot, and the captain was killed with number six shot. So the murderer took the number sevens and replaced them with the number sixes he had brought with him.

'Then he had to get rid of the grouse, otherwise the police would wonder why his gun was still loaded *after* the captain had got his brace. He took them from the bag and hid them in the heather. He should have hidden them farther away, but maybe he wanted to rush back and get into his bed before the household was awake.

'What the police found was a dead man full of number six shot, two spent number six cartridges in his gun, and more number sixes in his pocket. The murderer was sure everyone would think it was accidental death. It should have been the perfect murder.' He glanced sharply at the faces turned towards him, faces that were no longer looking to Blair for help. They all looked shocked and strained.

'But the fence and the feather in the game bag made me suspicious, so I arranged with Angus and our dogs to do a bit of tracking this morning. We backtracked over the captain's trail, in the direction away from the castle and, sure enough, we found the freshly used cartridges, number sevens. It took us a couple of hours, tracking in increasing circles away from the spot where the body was found, to find the grouse.

'I think that when the birds are examined, it'll be found they were shot around the morning of the twelfth and that they were killed with number seven shot.'

'It's still all speculation,' said Blair furiously.

'I should suppose,' said Hamish. 'that his gear is still in his room and his car is still out front. I suggest we search both and see if he had any more cartridges with him.'

'Go and have a look, Jenkins,' barked the colonel.

'This is all a muddle, you village idiot,' said Blair, turning a dangerous colour of puce. 'You keep calling the murderer a "he". How do you know it was a man?'

'I don't,' said Hamish. 'It could just as easily have been a woman.'

Voices rose in a furious buzz. 'He's a better fiction writer than I am,' came Henry's sharp tones. And Mrs Halburton-Smythe's voice, shaky with tears: 'This is a nightmare. You must stop Macbeth making up these lies, Priscilla.'

Jenkins came back into the room, carrying a small box. He handed it to Colonel Halburton-Smythe. The colonel opened it and looked gloomily down at the contents. 'Number seven,' he said in a hollow voice.

Everyone looked at Blair again as if he were their last hope. Hamish studied their faces. They were all, even Priscilla, willing Blair to say that Hamish Macbeth had made a mistake.

But Blair's heavy head was down on his chest. 'I'll need to call the boys in,' he mumbled.

'Speak up!' demanded Lord Helmsdale.

'I'll need tae get statements from ye,' roared Blair suddenly, making them all jump. 'This is a bad business. And you'll all need tae stay here until your rooms are searched. Come wi' me, sir,' he said to the colonel.

The colonel followed him out. The rest stayed where they were, stricken, looking accusingly at Hamish, and listening to the mumble of voices from the hall.

Blair was in a quandary. He sweated to think what his superiors would say if they learned he had been made to look a fool by the local bobby. But if he could get Hamish out of the investigation before anyone from Strathbane arrived, then he could make it look as if he, as a diligent officer, had been unsatisfied with the accident verdict and had returned to the scene of the crime.

'Look here, sir,' he said in oily, wheedling tones. 'This is going to take a wee bit of time. Now I am sure you don't want the television and press to harass your wife, daughter, or guests. If you would let me set up headquarters here with MacNab and Anderson, we'll soon get to the bottom of this.'

'You'll find this dreadful murder had nothing to do with me or my guests,' said Colonel Halburton-Smythe.

'Exactly,' cried Blair. 'And you won't want your family or guests troubled with a lot of haranguing, which they would get if they allowed that Macbeth to stay around.'

The colonel hesitated. In all fairness, he could hardly bring himself to agree with the detective inspector's description of Macbeth's possible line of questioning. It was Blair who was notorious for his bullying manner. But Blair now seemed conciliatory and was behaving in a servile manner – which was more the way the man ought to behave, thought the colonel. He knew Hamish Macbeth would suspect each and every one of the guests. And Hamish, never as overawed by the local gentry as the colonel thought he ought to be, would not dream of taking the heat away from the castle by questioning the locals first. Then there was Priscilla to consider. The colonel, deep down, had always feared that one day Priscilla might horrify them by upping and saying she wished to marry the village policeman. It was only a half-formulated idea, never openly admitted, for the colonel was too much of a snob to bring that thought out into the open and look at it. But it niggled away at the back of his mind. Then there was the final clincher. If it hadn't been for Macbeth's interference, this sordid death would still be considered a respectable and gentlemanly accident – which Colonel Halburton-Smythe was still convinced it was. He found himself saying that Blair could stay at Tommel Castle, provided he agreed to keep the press at bay.

'But don't go upsetting the servants, mind,' said the colonel. 'No ringing the bells and making them fetch and carry. It's hard enough to get good servants these days. I don't want them handing in their notice because some copper decides to behave like a lord of the manor.'

Blair bit back an angry retort and bared his teeth in a horrible fawning smile instead.

In his new cringing manner, he thanked the colonel profusely and then went back to the breakfast room and jerked his head at Hamish as a signal that the policeman was to follow him out into the hall.

'Not here,' said Hamish, seeing Jenkins lurking in a corner of the hall. 'You're chust dying to have a go at me. Let's go outside.'

He walked ahead out of the castle, and with a muttered curse, Blair followed him.

Hamish walked up to his car and then turned and faced the detective inspector. 'Out wi' it, man,' he said laconically.

Blair took a deep breath.

'In the first place, Officer,' he snarled, 'You

are incorrectly dressed. I shall put in a report about that.'

Hamish was wearing a worn checked shirt and an old pair of flannel trousers.

'Secondly, I am still convinced that this was an accident. You had no right to crawl about the moors looking for clues wi'out phoning me and telling me what you were doing. Thirdly, you should not have sent that helicopter pilot off before I saw him. You're standing there, you big scunner, thinking you're cleverer than me because you think you solved that last case. Well, it was a fluke, see. It's all going in my report, and I'll see you in front of a police committee yet, you cheeky bugger.'

'Aye, well,' said Hamish amiably, 'that would be the terrible thing. I can see it now,' he went on dreamily, 'telling all the bigwigs how Detective Chief Inspector Blair wanted to let a murder pass as an accident. I'm wearing my old clothes because that uniform of mine can't stand much more –'

'Whit?' roared Blair. 'Listen, laddie, I happen to know you had the money for a new uniform last year.'

Hamish bit his lip. He had not spent the money on a new uniform, but had sent it home to his family.

'Anyway,' said Hamish airily with a wave of his hand, 'to get to the matter of the helicopter pilot. His name's Billy Simpson and I typed out his statement and you can have it today. In any case, his statement doesn't matter now, for the pathologist's report says the captain died before the helicopter arrived. But I can tell all this to that police committee you were threatening me with.'

'Maybe I was a bit hasty,' said Blair. 'We'll forget about the pilot. Just you run along and look after all those interesting cases like kiddies nicking sweets from the local shop and leave the big stuff to the experts.'

'I was at a party here the night before the shooting,' said Hamish. 'I could describe what the guests were like and how they behaved to the captain.'

Blair clapped him on the shoulder. 'Maybe I'll drop down to the station and get it from ye later.'

'So I'm not to have the honour of putting you up?' said Hamish.

Blair puffed out his chest. 'I'll be staying here at the castle. The colonel's invitation.'

Hamish looked amused.

'So just run along and keep out of it,' said Blair.

'Aye, wi' an expert like yourself around,' sighed Hamish, 'you won't be needing me.'

He opened the car door. 'Don't forget to get the grouse examined,' he said.

Blair grunted and turned to walk away.

'And don't forget the gun room,' said Hamish sweetly.

Blair swung about.

'What?'

'The gun room ... in the castle,' said Hamish patiently. 'Someone shot the captain, and unless they were silly enough to have the gun lying about their bedroom, you'll probably find a gun has been borrowed from the gun room, cleaned, and put back.'

Police Constable Macbeth drove sedately out of the estate and along the road to Lochdubh. He pulled to the side of the road at the top of the hill overlooking the village, switched off the engine, and climbed out of the car.

A mist was rising from the loch below, lifting and falling. One minute the village lay in its neat two rows, and the next was blotted from view.

'I hate that man!' cried Hamish loudly. A startled sheep skittered off on its black legs.

He took a great gulp of fresh air. Hamish hardly ever lost his temper, but Blair's dismissal of him from the case was infuriating. Hamish, in that brief moment, hated not only Blair but Priscilla Halburton-Smythe as well. She was nothing but a silly girl who had become engaged to a man simply because he was famous. She was not worth a single moment's heartbreak. And let Blair solve the case if he could!

Hamish reminded himself fiercely that he had settled for a quiet life. He had had chances of promotion and had sidestepped them all, for he knew he would find life in a large town unpleasant. He would need to obey his superiors who might turn out to be like Blair. He loved his easy, lazy life and the beauty of the countryside. Apart from his hens and geese, he rented a piece of croft land behind the police station where he kept sheep. There was enough to be made on the side in Lockdubh, what with the egg money, the sale of lambs, and the money prizes he won at the various Highland games. Why should he throw it all away out of hurt pride – because a detective had insulted him and the daughter of the castle had made it obvious she enjoyed money and fame, even if that fame was only reflected glory?

His anger went as quickly as it had come, leaving him feeling tired and sad.

He climbed back in his car, stopping outside Lochdubh to give a lift to a sticky urchin who had wandered too far from home.

Once inside the police station, which had an office on one side, with one cell, and the living quarters on the other, he hung a notice on the door referring all inquiries to Strathbane police, and then went inside and firmly locked and bolted it.

The newspapers and television would be along soon, and Hamish knew that ordinary constables were not supposed to give statements to the press. It was easier to pretend he was not at home instead of having to open the door every five minutes to say, 'No comment.'

He ate a late breakfast, and then, taking Towser, decided to walk about the village and make sure all was quiet. Murder at the castle should not distract him from more petty crimes. The crimes committed in the village were usually drunkenness, petty shoplifting, and wife-beating – or husband-beating. Drugs had not yet reached this remote part of north-west Scotland.

He went on his rounds, dropping into various cottages for cups of tea. Then he ambled along to the Lochdubh Hotel to pass the time of day with Mr Johnson, the hotel manager.

'What's this I'm hearing?' said Mr Johnson, ushering Hamish into the gloom of the hotel office. 'They're saying it's a murder up at Tommel.'

'You get the news quickly,' said Hamish.

'It was that Jessie. Does she ever do any work? She's always down in the village, mooning over that boyfriend of hers. She says the Mafia wasted Captain Bartlett – there was another American movie showing at the village hall the other night. *The Godfather*, I think it was.'

'No, it wisnae the Mafia,' said Hamish with a grin. 'I won't be having anything to do with the case. It's that scunner Blair from Strathbane. He told me to push off.'

'Blair doesn't know his arse from his elbow,' said Mr Johnson roundly. The bell rang on the reception desk outside. He hurried to answer it. Hamish listened, amused, to the sudden horrible refinement of the hotel manager's accent. 'Oh, yes, Major Finlayson, sir,' twittered Mr Johnson. 'We have a very good cellar, and Monsieur Pierre, our *maître d'*, will be delighted to discuss our wine list with you. Is modom well? Good, good. Grand day for the fishing, ha, ha.'

'Silly old fart,' said the manager, walking into the office and shutting the door. 'I hate wine snobs.'

'Who in the name o' the wee man is Monsieur Pierre?' asked Hamish.

'Och, it's Jimmy Cathcart from Glasgow. He thought it would look better if he pretended to be French. Mind you, when we get the French tourists, he says he's American. Now, what about this murder, Hamish?'

Hamish looked hopefully towards the coffee machine in the corner.

Mr Johnson took the hint and poured him out a cup.

Hamish sat down, nursing his cup of coffee, and described his findings.

'But you can't just leave it there!' exclaimed Mr Johnson when Hamish had finished.

'It is not my murder. It is Blair's.'

'Good heavens! That man couldn't find his own hands if they weren't attached to his arms. Are you going to let a murderer roam around on the loose? He might murder again.'

'It's not my case,' said Hamish stubbornly. He drank his coffee in one gulp and put the cup down on the desk. 'To tell you the truth, I no longer care if the whole damn lot of them up at that castle drop dead tomorrow.'

Chapter Seven

*. . . one of those people who would be
enormously improved by death.*
— Saki

By early evening, the mist had thickened.
Hamish was able to make out some figures
clustered around the outside of the police
station. He quietly made his way around to the
back door so as to avoid the gentlemen of
the press.

The thick mist had blotted out all sound.
Hamish fried a couple of herring for his dinner and gave Towser a bowl of Marvel Dog, a
new dog food given to him free by the local
shop to try out. Towser ate a mouthful and
then tottered around the kitchen, making dismal retching sounds.

'What a clown you are,' said Hamish. 'You
know I brought home some liver just in case
you didn't like Marvel Dog. Sit yourself down
until it's cooked.'

He had been feeling calm and peaceful just before his return home, but as he lifted down the heavy frying pan – Towser liked his liver medium rare – he was overcome by another wave of sadness. Was this what the future held for him? Chatting away in the evenings to a spoilt mongrel?

There came a sharp, impatient knocking on the front door. Hamish hesitated. He began to wonder if his relative, Rory Grant, who worked in London for the *Daily Chronicle*, had perhaps been sent up to cover the murder. He should have phoned Rory, he thought. It was too early perhaps for the Fleet Street boys to have arrived, unless Blair had released the news very quickly and some of them had managed to fly up from London.

He put the pan on the stove and dumped the liver into it and then cautiously tiptoed his way to the front door. He pulled aside the lace curtain at the window at the side of the door. In the misty half-light, he could just make out the sharp features of Detective Jimmy Anderson, Blair's underling.

Cursing his own curiosity, he unlocked the door. 'Come in quickly,' said Hamish. 'I've been avoiding the press.'

'They've had short shrift from Blair,' said Anderson. 'But headquarters in Strathbane phoned the news of the murder to the local paper after Blair told them about it. They'll have phoned Fleet Street. The Scottish television stations are here and all the Scottish papers from Dumfries to John o'Groats. You'd think they'd never had a murder in Scotland before.'

'It's a rich-folks' murder,' said Hamish, 'and that makes a world o' difference. Come in.'

Anderson followed Hamish into the kitchen and stood watching as Hamish seized the frying pan and turned the liver over.

'That smells good,' said Anderson. 'Sorry to interrupt your dinner.'

'It's no' for me,' said Hamish, blushing. 'It's fur ma dog.'

'I bet ye buy it presents for its birthday,' jeered Anderson.

'Don't be daft,' said Hamish furiously, remembering with shame that he had bought Towser a new basket for his birthday just last month. 'What brings you here?'

'The fact is,' said Anderson, 'I could do with a dram.'

'Oh, aye? And you staying in splendour at Tommel Castle.'

'I rang the bell to ask for a drink,' said Anderson, his sharp blue eyes roaming about the kitchen as if searching for a whisky bottle, 'and that berk, Jenkins, answered. "Police are not to ring bells for the servants," he says. "I'll remember that, mac," says I. "Just fetch me a drink." "Colonel Halburton-Smythe's instructions," says he, "but the officers of the law are not to imbibe intoxicating liquor while on duty and will take their meals in the servants' hall." I told thon old ponce where he could put his servants' meals and he told the colonel, who told Blair, and Blair's gone all creepy and told me I'd better take a walk until he calmed the colonel down.'

'I might have something,' said Hamish, piling the liver into Towser's bowl. 'Then again, I might not.'

'I thought,' said Anderson, staring at the ceiling, 'that perhaps you might like to get a run-down on all the statements.'

'I'm not on the case,' said Hamish, 'but come through to the living room and I'll see what I can do.'

Hamish's living room was not often used. It did not even boast a television set. Bookshelves lined the walls, and the mantelpiece was crammed with various trophies, which Anderson examined. 'You seem to have won everything,' he commented. 'Hill running, clay-pigeon shooting, angling competition, even chess! Bring in much money?'

'The hill running does, and the angling.' said Hamish, 'and sometimes the shooting if it's at a big game fair. But often the prize is something like a salmon or a bottle of whisky.'

He took out a glass and began to fill it with whisky.

'Steady on,' said Anderson. 'I'll need some water in that.'

114

'It's watered already,' said Hamish, 'and don't ask me why, for I cannae be bothered telling you.' For although Hamish did not mind discussing the laird's wife's penchant for topping up the prize bottles of whisky with water with the locals or Priscilla, he had no intention of running down the good lady's reputation to an outsider.

'Here's to you,' said Anderson. 'Round the wallies, round the gums, look out, stomach, here it comes.'

'Chust so,' said Hamish stolidly. He studied Anderson covertly. Anderson was a thin, restless man with oily fair hair and a discontented foxy face. Of the three, Blair, McNab, and Anderson, Hamish had, in the past, found Anderson the most approachable.

'The last thing,' said Anderson, 'that I heard before I left was that forensics had taken a gun out of the gun room. It was a John Rigby. They've taken it back to Strathbane to double-check, but they're sure as anything it was cleaned right after the murder. Could the murderer have switched cartridges, seeing as how Bartlett had a Purdey and he had a John Rigby?'

'The Rigby's a twelve-bore, isn't it?' asked Hamish.

Anderson nodded.

'Any twelve-bore cartridge goes into any twelve-bore gun.'

'How long would it take to clean a shot-gun?'

'About five minutes,' said Hamish. 'You put a little gun-cleaning fluid into each barrel and then you scrub the inside of each barrel with a phosphor-bronze brush. Then you put a patch on the jag – that's a wee piece of flannelette on a rod sort of thing – and you push that through the barrels. If you're doing the job properly, you finish it off with gun oil on a lamb's-wool mop, go over the extractors with a toothbrush to remove any powder that may have got caught, and then go over the metal parts of the gun with an oily cloth. I suppose they've dusted the gun-cleaning equipment for prints?'

'A set of gun-cleaning thingumajigs has gone, says the colonel. And it'll not surprise you to learn there were no prints on the gun.'

'Checked everyone's clothes for oil?'

'Not a sign of it. Even Pomfret's clothes are clean, and you'd expect his shooting clothes would have some oil on them.'

'I think our murderer must have been used to shooting,' said Hamish cautiously.

'Why? It doesn't take much expertise to go right up to someone and blow a hole in his chest.'

'Well,' sighed Hamish, 'here's what I'm thinking. I don't believe the murderer could have counted on the captain being conveniently at that fence and in the perfect position to fake a suicide. An amateur might just have loaded two cartridges into the gun before going out. A man used to shooting would automatically fill his pockets with cartridges. The murderer had enough cartridges with him to change his for the captain's – I mean not only in the gun, but in the captain's pockets as well. Anyway, we know how it was done. The question is – why? How well did they all know him?'

'Oh, they all knew him, all right. Seems they've run into him at various house parties. Everyone very vague. Miss Smythe is the only one who's definite in her statement. She said she met him two years ago when she and some of her friends went to the Highland Dragoons' annual rifle shoot. She is also the only one who seems to have liked him.

'Jessica Villiers and Diana Bryce came in to see Blair together. He told Jessica to go and Diana to stay. The girls exchanged sort of conspiratorial, warning looks. Diana starts patronizing Blair. "One meets the same people over and over again in our set, but I don't suppose someone like you is aware of that" type of thing. Jessica is called in and says the same thing. Blair blows his top and starts bullying them and everyone else. Everyone clams up on the spot. Captain Bartlett could be offensive, they say, but not as offensive as *some* – meaning Blair, of course. Blair is also high-handed with the servants. Servants who might be the

117

gossipy type clam up on the spot and play the old retainer bit.'

'And who is the chief suspect?' asked Hamish, rising and filling up Anderson's glass.

'Thanks. Well, the chief suspect is Jeremy Pomfret. He's the one who had the bet with Bartlett.'

'Dearie me,' said Hamish. 'Mr Pomfret has pots of money, and five thousand pounds to him would be like a five-pound note to me.'

'Okay, Sherlock, who would you pick?'

'I think there's a lot of them with motives,' said Hamish. 'I was at a party at the castle the night before the shooting. One minute Vera Forbes-Grant was drooling over Bartlett, and the next, she'd flung her drink in his face. Jessica and Diana had their heads together and they were staring at the captain in hate and horror, as if they'd just learned something awful. Diana started to yak to me about how easy it is to die from an accident in the Highlands, and when I said I was the local bobby, she clammed up. I think Freddy Forbes-Grant knows his wife had an affair with Bartlett. I think Sir Humphrey Throgmorton has reason to hate Bartlett as well. The Helmsdales didn't like him either. Henry Withering knew him. How well, I don't know.

'As for Jeremy Pomfret, he wanted me to come up to the castle and referee the shoot, but I had to tell him the colonel wouldnae stand

118

for that. He didn't trust Bartlett and he didn't like him.'

'What I don't understand,' said Anderson, 'is that this house party is supposed to be so that the chosen few can meet the famous playwright. But most of them seem to have a grudge against Bartlett, and all seem to have known him. Weird that they should all end up at the same house party.'

'Not really,' said Hamish. 'Diana was right about meeting the same people. These landed gentry only visit each other, you know, and there's not that many folk this far north, so it stands to reason you'd end up running into the same people over and over again. I thought you would have known that.'

'Not me,' grinned Anderson. 'You don't often get crime in such elevated circles. The only highfalutin one I was ever on was that fishing one last year, but they were all visitors. I'm a town man, and there's usually plenty in Strathbane to keep us busy, what with keeping an eye on thae Russians from the Eastern Bloc fleet and trying to smash the poaching gangs. We've got those big council estates and most of the folks are unemployed and as tight as ticks with booze from one week's end to the other.'

'What about the paraffin test?' asked Hamish suddenly.

'Oh, to see if anyone had fired a gun recently? They don't use the paraffin test any more. They took swabs from everyone's hands and they've taken them back to the lab for tests. But they're pretty sure the murderer was wearing gloves.'

'So you're looking for the gloves?'

'Everyone's going to be up at dawn, combing the grounds,' yawned Anderson. 'Then we're checking up on all the guests. We'll soon be getting reports from all over. They're a cagey lot. They must know we'll find out all about them sooner or later, so you'd think they'd come clean.'

'With someone like Chief Inspector Blair, it's a pleasure not to help him in anything,' said Hamish.

'He's not bad when you get to know him. He's awf'y good at routine work. This is a bit out of his league.'

Hamish picked up the whisky bottle and put it away in a cupboard. Anderson cast a longing look after it before getting to his feet. 'Will I pass on to Blair what you said about the motives?' he asked.

Hamish thought of Blair, and then reminded himself severely there was a murderer at large. He shrugged. 'Why not?' he said.

'I'll drop along tomorrow evening,' said Anderson, 'and let you know how things are going.'

'Aye, well, that would be grand,' said Hamish reluctantly. He had a very human longing to leave Blair to his own devices and watch him make a muck of the case.

After Anderson had left, Hamish began to wonder if he would be any better than Blair at finding out who the murderer was. And the more he wondered, the more his curiosity took over from his hurt at Blair's snub.

He went into his office. There would be no harm in making a few calls to various friends and relatives. Like many Highlanders, Hamish had relatives scattered all over the world, and he was thankful he still had a good few of the less ambitious ones in different parts of Scotland.

He walked over to the wall where there was a large faded map of the north of Scotland and gazed at the county of Caithness, finally pinpointing the Bryces' and Villierses' estates.

The nearest town to both was Lybster. He sat down at his desk and phoned his fourth cousin, Diarmuid Grant, who had a croft outside Lybster. The conversation took over an hour. Things could not be hurried. There was the weather to be discussed, the decline in the grouse population, the vagaries of tourists, the price of sheep at the Lairg sales, the welfare of Diarmuid's large brood of children, before the backgrounds of Jessica Villiers and Diana Bryce could be gone into.

By the time he put down the phone, Hamish was conscious of a feeling of excitement. He may as well, he thought, put through a few more calls and find out what he could about the other members of the house party.

By eleven o'clock, he had only gone halfway down the list.

He decided to leave the rest until the morning.

The next day was calm and quiet, 'a nice soft day' as they say in Scotland, which means a warm and weeping drizzle.

There was no news from the castle. Even Jessie failed to appear in the village. Hamish politely dealt with any members of the press who turned up. He considered 'No comment' too rude a form of dismissal for his Highland taste, served anyone who arrived at the police station with strong tea and biscuits, and sent them on their way to Tommel Castle, turning a deaf ear to their complaints that they had already been there and had been turned away at the gates.

He called in at the grocers-cum-hardware-cum-post-office-cum-off-licence for a bottle of good whisky in anticipation of Anderson's promised evening visit. He made various phone calls to friends and relatives around Scotland and then to Rory Grant on the *Daily Chronicle* in London. Satisfied he had collected enough to open up several new angles in the case, he settled down to wait for Anderson.

But the long quiet day dripped its way into darkness and there was no sign of the detective.

Again, Hamish felt anger rising up inside him. A proper superior officer would at least have had him out searching the moors for clues instead of leaving him in such isolation.

He tried to forget about the case, but his mind kept turning over what he had heard on the phone and what he had overheard at the party.

Hamish usually preferred warm bottled beer as a drink, but that evening he found himself opening up the bottle he had bought to entertain Anderson and pouring himself a hefty measure.

Soothed at last by the spirit, he was able to convince himself he was better off out of the case. Surely Blair, with the whole forensic team and two detectives to help him, would produce something.

But the next morning he awoke to a day of wind and glitter. A warm gale was blowing in from the Gulf Stream, carrying snatches of voices and strains of radio music from the nearby houses. The sun sparkled on the choppy waters of Lochdubh, hurting Hamish's eyes as he struggled out to feed the hens and geese. A sea-gull floated with insolent ease near his head, eyeing the buckets of feed with one prehistoric eye. In the field behind the police station, rabbits scampered for shelter, and up against the blinding blue of the sky, rooks were being tossed by buffets of wind like bundles of black rags. It was a day of false spring, a day of anticipation, a day when you felt that if something did not happen soon, you would burst. Streams of peat-smoke rushed down from the chimney, to be shredded by the minor gales blowing around the corner of the station. Hamish, like most of the villagers, kept the kitchen fire going winter and summer because the hot water was supplied from a boiler at the back of the hearth.

The one nagging fact that there was a murderer on the loose and that he was not being allowed to do anything about it returned to plague him.

Hamish collected the eggs from the hen-house and returned to the kitchen. Someone was knocking loudly on the door of the police station.

Expecting a hung-over member of the press, Hamish went to open it.

Anderson stood on the step, a wide grin on his face.

'You're to come with me, Macbeth,' he said.

'Where?' asked Hamish.

'To the castle. Blair's been deposed.'

'Come in and wait till I put my uniform on,' said Hamish. 'What happened?'

Anderson followed him into the bedroom.

'Well, you ken how Blair's been oiling and creeping around the colonel ...'

'I didn't,' said Hamish. 'You just said he'd turned creepy.'

'Aye, well, he's been touching his forelock to the colonel while snapping and bullying the guests. I told him what you had said, and he lost his temper and insisted on keeping them all up half the night. Turns out the colonel roused the Chief Constable out of his bed and read the riot act and the Chief roused the Super at Strathbane out of *his* bed and read the dot act, so at dawn Chief Superintendent John Chalmers arrives and rouses *us* up out of our beds. Why had Blair subjected possibly innocent people to such a grilling? Because, says Blair, of vital new evidence. Where did said evidence come from? From the local bobby, chips in I. Where is said local bobby? Dismissed from the case, says Miss Priscilla Halburton-Smythe, appearing in a dressing gown, because Hamish Macbeth is too highly intelligent a man for Inspector Blair, she says nastily, and if you ask her opinion, Blair wants said Macbeth off said murder in case said Macbeth solves it. Get Macbeth, says the Super, and sends Blair out to join the common bobbies who are ploughing through the heather still looking for that gun-cleaning outfit. So here I am.'

Hamish laughed. 'I'd love to see Blair's face. But will he no' make life a misery for you when this case is over?'

'No,' said Anderson. 'I'm a bigger creep than Blair, and I'll toady so much, he'll forget about the whole thing.'

'Nearly ready,' said Hamish, buttoning his tunic.

'What about a bit o' breakfast?' wheedled Anderson. 'They're not going to give us time to have any when we get to the castle.'

Hamish made bacon-and-egg baps and tea, eating his own breakfast in record time and then standing impatiently over Anderson until the detective had finished.

He agreed to go in Anderson's car, leaving Towser to roam the garden.

'Find out anything more?' asked Anderson.

'Aye,' said Hamish. 'A lot more. I tell you this, Jimmy Anderson, it's a fair wonder someone waited this long to murder Bartlett!'

Chapter Eight

Boundless intemperance
In nature is a tyranny, it hath been
The untimely emptying of the happy throne,
And the fall of many kings.

                                        – Shakespeare

Superintendent John Chalmers looked like an
ageing bank clerk. He was tall and thin, with
grey hair and watery blue eyes that peered
warily out at the world as if expecting another
onslaught of the slings and arrows of out-
rageous fortune. He had a small black moustache like a postage stamp above a rabbity
mouth. His ears stuck out like jug handles, as
if God had specially made them that way to
support his bowler hat.

He had been out in the grounds somewhere
and was returning to the castle when Hamish
and the detective arrived.

He greeted Hamish courteously and asked
him to accompany him into the castle.

The colonel had given up his study to the

police. It was a dim little room filled with the clutter of a man who had lost interest in field sports some years ago. Dusty game bags were thrown in one corner under shelves of Badminton Library books on hunting, shooting and fishing. A pair of green wellington boots held a selection of fishing rods.

There was an unusual stuffed fox in a glass case. It was lying down on its side, looking as if it had been sleeping peacefully at the time it was shot. The superintendent looked down at it sadly for several moments before taking off his bowler hat, polishing it with his sleeve and hanging it on one of the fishing rods.

He sat down behind a battered wooden desk, waved Hamish into a chair opposite, and said to Anderson, who was hovering in the doorway, 'Go down to the kitchens and question the servants again. See if you can get them to like you. People will not talk if you put their backs up.'

When Anderson had gone, he turned to Macbeth. 'Now, Constable,' he said, 'it looks as if we'll need to start again from the beginning. The people at this house party are very upset and claim they have been treated badly. I do not know if that is true or not, but we'll soon find out. I gather from Anderson that you know a little about the guests?'

'I know quite a lot more now,' said Hamish. 'I made various phone calls to find out about their backgrounds.'

'We now have several reports coming in from different police stations. Ah, here is PC Macpherson, who will take the shorthand notes. Now, the first one who's agreed to be interviewed all over again is Colonel Halburton-Smythe. Having dragged me into the case, he is naturally now anxious to be as helpful as possible. You listen closely to my line of questioning, and if there's something you know that we don't know, I shall expect you to step in and put in your own questions. Take that chair over by the window and look as unobtrusive as possible.'

Macpherson went to fetch the colonel, who soon came bustling in. He looked taken aback to see Hamish there, but after a little hesitation he sat down and faced the superintendent.

The colonel appeared pleased to answer the series of polite and simple questions. He said the party had gone on much later than they had expected – until two in the morning. No one had therefore been up and about around the time the captain was supposed to have gone out on the moors. Yes, he had known about the bet with Pomfret, but not about Bartlett's deal with the Arabs. The guns in the gun room had not been used since last season. This August, Bartlett and Pomfret had brought their own guns.

Hamish remained quietly in his chair, looking out of the window, which faced on to the front of the castle.

The colonel ended by saying that Henry Withering and his daughter wanted to be interviewed next, as they were going out for the day.

The colonel went out and Henry Withering came in. He was wearing a lovat green sweater over a checked shirt and cavalry-twill trousers. He seemed composed and anxious to be helpful.

No, he said, he hadn't a clue who would want to bump off poor Peter. Mind you, he went on, there was no denying Peter was a terror with the ladies and had a way of putting people's backs up.

'And do you have a gun yourself, Mr Withering?' asked Chalmers.

There was a slight pause while Henry studied his nails. 'I've got one somewhere,' he said eventually. 'Probably at home at my parents' place in Sussex.'

'Are you a good shot?'

'Never was much good,' said Henry. 'Can I go now?'

'Just a little longer,' said Chalmers soothingly. 'How well did you know Captain Bartlett?'

'Well, I used to run into him a lot. He spent a little time in London before he rejoined his regiment. One meets the same people at parties and that sort of thing.'

'By parties, I assume you mean social parties?'

'Yes.'

'But it appears that, until recently, you did not go to social events. You are on record as saying you despised them.'

Henry laughed. 'Very possibly.' he said. 'I usually tell the press what they want to hear. But one went just the same.'

'I don't know,' said Chalmers cautiously, 'that I would say it was the press exactly, meaning the mass media. No one had heard of you until recently. But I believe you wrote an article once for *The Liberated Workers' World*.'

'One says silly things in one's youth.'

'This was three years ago.'

'Look,' said Henry with an engaging smile, 'I'm afraid I'm a bit of a fraud. I had to go along with all that left-wing stuff simply because you have to be left-wing to get your plays put on. The big theatres only take trash. You've no idea what it's like to sweat your guts out on a play and then find no one wants to put it on.'

'So you only knew Captain Bartlett as someone you bumped into at parties?'

'Absolutely.'

'You must, on the other hand,' said Hamish Macbeth softly, 'haff seen a good bit of the captain when you were both sharing that flat off Sloane Square. That would be two years ago.'

'Not really,' said Henry, not looking at Hamish, but continuing to smile at the superintendent. 'I said he could share my digs when

131

he was up in London, that sort of thing. I was away in the provinces most of the time. I came back to find the place a mess and that he'd been using my phone to call someone in the States. I left his suitcase with the porter at the block of flats and changed the locks.'

'Nonetheless, Mr Withering,' said the superintendent severely, 'you said nothing in your earlier statement about having known Captain Bartlett particularly well.'

'I didn't,' said Henry. 'Casual acquaintance, that's all.'

Chalmers took him slowly and carefully over all the things Henry had said in his earlier statement, congratulated him politely on his forthcoming marriage, and told him to tell Miss Halburton-Smythe to step along.

'You've been busy, Constable,' said Chalmers when Henry had left the room. 'How did you find out Bartlett had been staying with him?'

'I have a relative who works for the *Daily Chronicle*,' said Hamish. 'He asked the man who runs the social column about Bartlett. Seems this social editor has a memory like an elephant and he had written an article on Captain Bartlett, calling him the everlasting debs' delight. It appears that part of doing the Season was to have an affair with Peter Bartlett. He had been an indefatigable debchaser since he was a young man. A merry life o' broken hearts and paternity suits.'

'Was he attractive?'

'Aye, he was a fine-looking man, a bit like a fillum star. I suppose you've had the forensic results of the swabs taken from everyone's hands?'

'Yes, they're all as clean as a whistle. We had a bit of excitement over the results of Pomfret's swabs, but he turns out to be a heavy smoker and it can often turn up almost the same results. I understand it was you who discovered it was murder, not accident.'

'Did Mr Blair tell you that?'

'No, it was Colonel Halburton-Smythe. Much as he dislikes Blair, he is confident that an expert like myself will soon prove Blair was right and you were wrong.'

Hamish grinned. 'And if it hadnae been for my interference, they could all have been feeling comfy?'

'Something like that.'

Priscilla Halburton-Smythe walked into the room. She was wearing a dark red silk blouse with a cream pleated skirt. Her smooth blonde hair was curled in at the ends.

Superintendent John Chalmers looked at her with approval.

He took her through her statement, ticking off each point. Then he half-turned and looked expectantly at Hamish.

And for the first time, the superintendent began to have serious doubts about Hamish's intelligence. The constable was sitting staring vacantly into space, a half-smile curling his lips.

Chalmers frowned. The minute he had heard of this village constable and of how competently he had outlined how the murder had been done, he had lost no time in sending Anderson to fetch him. Unlike Blair, Chalmers was only interested in results. The fact that this trait had elevated him to the rank of superintendent should have told Blair something.

Hamish was in the grip of a powerful fantasy. He could see it all as clear as day. He was accusing Henry Withering of the murder, and Priscilla was throwing herself into Hamish's arms for protection. Henry's face was distorted in a villainous sneer.

'Macbeth!'

Hamish came back to reality with a bump.

'Have you any questions to ask?'

Hamish shifted uncomfortably. 'Well, Miss Halburton-Smythe,' he said, not meeting Priscilla's clear gaze. 'I wass, as you know, at the party afore the morning the murder took place. I am surprised you have not mentioned in your statement that Mrs Forbes-Grant threw her drink at the captain.'

Priscilla flushed and looked uncomfortable. 'You must admit, when it came to women Peter was enough to try the patience of a saint,' she said. 'I assumed at the time he had made one of his off remarks. Earlier in the day, he told me my home was the most pretentious, uncomfortable slum he had ever had the ill luck to be billeted in. I nearly slapped his face. I suppose you could describe him, on the face of it, as a man who could hold his drink in that he never fell over or was sick over your shoes or anything like that. But when he'd had a couple, he would turn immediately from being a very charming and attractive man to a downright nasty one.'

'Had you known him particularly well before this visit?' asked the superintendent.

'If you mean, was I ever one of his victims, the answer is no. As I said in my earlier statement, I had met him from time to time during the shooting season at other people's houses.'

'And do you know how to handle a gun?'

'A shotgun? Yes.'

'And would you describe yourself as a good shot, Miss Halburton-Smythe?'

'Oh, no, Superintendent.' Priscilla suddenly smiled at Hamish. 'I'm certainly not in Hamish's class.'

'Hamish being . . .?'

'Police Constable Macbeth.'

One watery blue eye swivelled curiously in Hamish's direction. Hamish folded his arms and looked at the ceiling.

'That will be all for the moment,' said Chalmers, turning back to Priscilla. 'Do you know who's volunteered to be next?'

'Pruney ... I mean Miss Prunella Smythe. She wants to get it over with so that she can go down to the village and buy some things.'

'Very well. Send her in.'

'I suppose you're looking for a pair of gloves?' asked Hamish.

'Yes, we can't eliminate the guests simply because they passed the forensic test. There is evidence that our murderer was wearing gloves,' said Chalmers.

Pruney fluttered in and sat down, crouched in the chair in front of the superintendent, and stared at her shoes – which were of the Minnie Mouse variety – as if she had never really seen them before.

'Miss Smythe,' began the superintendent.

Pruney started violently, her handbag slid off her lap, she bent to retrieve it, and her thick glasses fell off her nose and landed with a clatter on the floor.

Hamish went to help her, but she brushed him away. She snatched at her handbag, which was upended on the floor, and all the contents spilled out. There was a small medicine bottle, a bunch of keys, eight hairpins, an old-fashioned powder compact, a romance entitled *Desert Passion*, and a tube of wine gums.

'Now, now,' said Hamish, gently taking hold of her frantically scrabbling hands, 'this is not the Gestapo. Chust sit yourself down and let me get these things.' Pruney retreated to the chair while Hamish carefully replaced all the items in her handbag and then popped her glasses back on her nose. 'Now, what about a cup of tea?' he asked.

Pruney gave him a watery smile. 'So kind,' she said. 'Really, it has all been too much for me. Poor Captain Bartlett. Such a fine man. Such a loss. No, I shall do very well now, thank you, Officer. Tea will not be necessary.'

Hamish retreated to his post by the window.

'I've been reading over your statement, Miss Smythe,' said Chalmers, 'and it is very clear and straightforward. I see no reason to keep you very long.'

He took her carefully back over her first meeting with the captain at the regimental rifle shoot, and then asked her gently if she had specifically come to the house party to meet him again.

'Oh, no,' exclaimed Pruney. 'It was Mr Withering I wanted to meet. I had seen his play in London, you know, and adored every word. The minute I heard Mary – that's Mrs Halburton-Smythe – was having him as a guest. I simply pleaded with her to ask me.'

'You appear to be the only person who has a good word to say for Captain Bartlett,' observed the superintendent.

'Indeed?' Pruney's round, ingenuous eyes looked at the superintendent and then at Hamish. 'I found him such a kind man. Mr Withering was unnecessarily sharp with me when I was only trying to be pleasant, and

Captain Bartlett was most comforting. That horrible man, Blair, accused me of having an affair with him. Me!' exclaimed Pruney, although she looked highly gratified.

'You strike me, Miss Smythe,' came Hamish's soft voice, 'as being the kind of lady who sees only the best in people.'

'I think that is surely a better attitude to life than always finding fault,' said Pruney, who was beginning to evince signs of enjoying herself.

'Aye, but that may mean you might have noticed a lot of useful clues without *knowing* they were useful,' said Hamish. 'What did you think, for example, of that incident at the party when Mrs Forbes-Grant threw her drink at the captain?'

'I thought she must be drunk,' said Pruney. 'Mrs Forbes-Grant loves sweet things. She is always eating cakes and chocolates, and when she drinks alcohol, she drinks awful things like rum and Coke or crème de menthe or sweet champagne, and I read a most fascinating article the other day which said that all that sugar puts the alcohol into the blood-stream quicker. It is not like the old days, you know. Ladies do drink an awful lot at house parties. I was at a party on the borders last year and a lady of my age lifted up her skirt and *snapped her garter*.'

'That's verra curious,' said Hamish with great interest, while the superintendent glared at him impatiently. 'I was not aware that ladies wore garters any more.'

'That's what I thought!" cried Pruney. 'But a most obliging gentleman at the party told me they sold them in naughty shops.' Her eyes gleamed behind her thick spectacles. 'I find gentlemen's attitudes to the changing fashions in ladies' underwear most interesting. Only the other week –'

'Quite,' said the superintendent repressively. 'To get back to that point the constable was making, can you tell us anything you might have overheard that struck you as curious?'

Pruney giggled and put her hands to her face. 'It's rather like gossiping in the dorm,' she said. 'Still, it *is* a murder investigation. There was just one little thing. I could not sleep and I went downstairs to look for a copy of *The Times* to do the crossword. I find *The Times* crossword quite soporific. As I was passing Captain Bartlett's room, I saw a light under the door.' Pruney blushed. 'I was about to knock, thinking he could not sleep either and might be glad of company, when I heard Mrs Forbes-Grant's voice very clearly. She said, "You can't have. Not you of all people. I don't believe a word of it." '

'And what did the captain reply to that?' asked Hamish.

'I could not hear. The doors are very thick,' said Pruney regretfully. 'He said something because there was a sort of masculine rumble.

139

Then I saw Miss Bryce walking along the passage towards me. She gave me a nasty look, as if I had been eavesdropping, which of course I hadn't, so I went on downstairs. When I came back up about ten minutes later, the light under the captain's door was out.'

'Did you hear anything else?' asked the superintendent.

Pruney wrinkled her brow. 'No,' she said at last.

'Perhaps you might remember something more,' said Hamish. 'You strike me as a highly observant lady.' Pruney preened. 'If anything comes to mind, tell me or the superintendent here.'

'I most certainly shall,' said Pruney, gathering up her handbag. 'I wouldn't tell that nasty man, Blair, anything. He is not a silly man, but overambitious. I am glad he has been toppled.' She smiled at them warmly and scurried out.

'We had better have Mrs Forbes-Grant in,' said the superintendent. 'See if you can find her, Macpherson. The minute that woman comes in here, I shall accuse her of having an affair with Captain Bartlett.'

'Do you think that's a good idea?' asked Hamish cautiously. 'People are no' ashamed o' infidelity these days. If you're kind and sympathetic, she may tell you herself.'

The superintendent shuffled his papers. Then he said mildly, 'You may be right.'

Hamish let out a slow sigh of relief. He sometimes wondered how many murderers escaped justice because of power struggles in the police department.

There was an altercation outside the door. It appeared that Freddy Forbes-Grant was insisting on being present while his wife was interviewed, and PC Macpherson was firmly refusing permission.

The superintendent was just rising from his seat to go to his constable's aid when Macpherson ushered Vera in.

She was the only member of the house party to have donned mourning. She was wearing a plain black suit with a necklace of seed pearls. Her thick dyed-blonde hair was simply styled and the severe cut of the suit flattered her figure.

There was a loose pouch of flesh under her chin, and a disappointed droop to her full mouth, but she was still, thought Hamish, a very sexy woman. Her large blue eyes looked pleadingly at the superintendent.

'I don't think I can take much more of this,' she said in her husky voice. 'The murder's bad enough without having to be dragged over and over every little bit of it.'

'We won't keep you long,' said Chalmers soothingly. He took her through her statement, and then said mildly he was surprised she had not told Mr Blair about throwing her drink at the captain.

'I lied to him,' said Vera defiantly. 'He kept shouting and shouting at me, so I thought it better to say nothing.'

'I apologize on behalf of the Strathbane police,' said Chalmers. 'No one is going to shout at you. You are a valuable witness. Now, what caused that scene?'

'Where I threw the drink at him?'

'Yes.'

Vera bit her full bottom lip. 'Look,' she said, 'he made a nasty remark about my hair. He said my roots were black. I was feeling tired and overwrought. My nerves are not very strong. The minute I had tossed the drink at him, I was so ashamed of having made a scene that I burst into tears and left the room.'

'And did he also make a remark about Miss Bryce and Miss Villiers?' asked Hamish.

'What?'

'Just before you threw your drink at him,' said Hamish, 'you were looking up at him and your lips were framing a kiss. He said something. You looked horrified. He turned and looked pointedly at Miss Bryce and Miss Villiers, then he turned back and gave you a knowing look, and he winked. *That* was when you threw your drink at him.'

'I don't know what you are talking about,' cried Vera, an ugly tide of red beginning to crawl up her neck.

'Mrs Forbes-Grant,' said Hamish in a soft voice. 'We are from the police department and not the Moral Rearmament. It would be quite easy, I think, to prove that you had an affair with Captain Bartlett. Now, that is your own business. You are a very beautiful woman and must often be plagued with men chasing you.'

Vera gulped and looked at Hamish, who gave her a charming smile.

'Freddy doesn't know,' she said. 'Freddy mustn't ever know.'

'And he won't,' said Hamish, 'unless it has a direct bearing on the murder. But it would be nice to get it out of the way. The only thing that's suspicious about it is your refusal to talk. You must see that.'

There was a long silence while Vera looked down at her plump hands on her lap.

'All right,' she said at last. 'I did have an affair with him a few years ago. I didn't know he was going to be here. He made me think he still loved me. I visited his room, the night before the party. He said . . . he said I couldn't stay the rest of the night or Freddy would find out. I thought he loved me. I was prepared to run away with him. He said . . . at the party . . . I hadn't been the only woman who had been in his room. I told him he was lying. And then he turned and looked at Diana and Jessica, and turned back to me and winked. I knew all in that moment – he'd used me as he'd used me before. I saw red. I must have been mad, because I can't afford to leave Freddy anyway.'

143

There was a long silence.

Chalmers said, 'How long have you been married to Mr Forbes-Grant?'

'Twenty years.'

'And he knew nothing of your affair with Captain Bartlett?'

'Oh, no. Freddy's quite stupid. But he can make money. That merchant bank of his is one of the most powerful in the country. He's more or less retired. He wanted to come and live up here and start afresh. The simple life,' said Vera with a harsh laugh. 'But he runs the bank by phone.'

'Where did your affair with Captain Bartlett take place?' asked Hamish.

'In London. Freddy was abroad. We keep a flat in Knightsbridge.'

'And did Captain Bartlett at any time suggest you leave your husband?'

'No. We were two of a kind. I used to give him money out of my allowance. It sounds awful now. Peter used to say I loved money more than men.'

'And is that true?' asked Hamish, genuinely curious.

'It's all men are good for in the long run,' said Vera. 'Oh, you occasionally meet some fellow and think it's springtime all over again. But nothing lasts ... except money.'

Chalmers cleared his throat. 'Can you use a shotgun, Mrs Forbes-Grant?'

Vera laughed. Hamish thought she looked like someone leaving the confessional. She had told the worst and now she could relax.

'No, I can't,' she said. 'But it doesn't take any expertise to blow a hole in someone at point-blank range. I could have done that.'

Chalmers patiently took her over the rest of her statement.

'You'd better see Freddy now,' said Vera, rising and smoothing down her skirt. 'You won't tell him . . .?'

Chalmers shook his head. 'Not unless it becomes necessary.'

'You mean, not unless one of us did the murder? Don't worry, Freddy couldn't kill a fly.'

She drifted out, leaving a heavy aroma of Arpège in the room behind her.

Freddy Forbes-Grant entered the room about a minute later.

It took ages to calm him down in order to get him to say anything coherent at all. But when he finally decided to talk reasonably, his statement had very little to add to what he had already said. Captain Bartlett had insulted his wife on the evening before the murder and had upset her terribly. She was not the only one Bartlett had upset. No, said Freddy, he did not believe in blood sports and never used a gun. They had more or less invited themselves to the Halburton-Smythes when they heard about Henry Withering. Both he and his wife had seen the play in London and thought it a rattling good show. He had written personally to the Secretary of State for Scotland to complain about Blair's harassment, and would complain again if Chalmers wasn't more careful and courteous. He, Freddy Forbes-Grant, considered all policemen some lower form of life anyway.

'He knows about his wife's affair,' said Hamish, after Freddy had crashed out.

'How do you make that out?' asked Chalmers.

'Thon is one very frightened man,' said Hamish. 'Something's terrifying him. I could smell him from here – fear-sweat. Angry, blustering, ranting people are usually frightened.'

'Like Colonel Halburton-Smythe?'

'Och, no. That one was born a scunner.'

Macpherson, who had left to find another victim, returned to say that no one else was available until the afternoon. They had either gone out or had sent messages via the servants to say they were not to be disturbed. Dr Brodie was with Sir Humphrey Throgmorton, who was in need of a sedative.

Chalmers turned to Hamish. 'In that case, you may as well tell me what you've discovered about the others.'

Hamish prised a small notebook out of his tunic pocket.

'Captain Bartlett,' he said, 'was having an affair with Jessica Villiers four years ago. He

146

met her friend, Diana, and dropped Jessica. He actually became engaged to Diana Bryce for two whole weeks before jilting her. The Helmsdales have reason to hate the captain. He turned up at a ball they were giving in their home near Dornoch with some other army officers. They got drunk and took the place apart. He painted a moustache on a portrait of a Helmsdale ancestor. The portrait was by Joshua Reynolds. The captain refused to pay for any of the damages. He went to sleep drunk with a cigarette burning in his hand and set his bedroom on fire. With the luck of the drunk, he jumped from his window on to the lawn and fell asleep again without warning anyone. The fire spread and burnt down most of the guest wing. It did not become a police matter, because Helmsdale inexplicably refused to prosecute. It came out later in county gossip that Helmsdale had fired a shotgun at the captain and missed. Captain Bartlett said if Helmsdale sued him, then he would sue Helmsdale for attempted manslaughter. It was at that point that Lady Helmsdale, beside herself with rage, punched Captain Bartlett and broke his jaw.'

'Golly!' said Chalmers. 'Don't tell me old Sir Humphrey has a reason to kill the captain as well?'

'He might have. He's a fanatical collector of rare china. He had some people to afternoon tea awhiles back and they brought along their houseguest, Captain Peter Bartlett. The poor old boy had the tea served in a very rare set. He went on bragging about the value and beauty of it. Captain Bartlett dropped his teacup and saucer on the hearth, smashing them and ruining the set.'

Chalmers sat for a long time deep in thought. Then he said, 'It's very curious that so many people with reason to hate Bartlett should be gathered together under one roof.'

'The British Isles is full of other people wi' mair reason to bump Bartlett off than any of the folks here,' said Hamish. 'I wass checking up all around. I am telling you this so's you will not be surprised when you get my phone bill. If we begin to think the murder was committed by someone outside the castle, then we are going to have a terrible job. There was a wee lassie in London killed herself with an overdose of sleeping pills when the captain jilted her, and then there's a lot of husbands as well who've threatened to kill him at one time or another.'

'Where did he get the stamina?' asked Chalmers in awe. 'Look at the evidence we've got from old Vera – three women in the one night.'

'He was supposed to have been one of those people who only need about four hours sleep a night,' said Hamish. 'And Captain Bartlett was always known as a Don Juan. Aye, it's an unfair world when you think of it. If that man had been a woman, he'd have been called a harlot!'

'Let's get back to Jeremy Pomfret,' said Chalmers, shuffling his papers. 'Did you unearth anything about him?'

'Nothing sinister,' said Hamish. 'He's rich, got an estate in Perthshire, met Bartlett from time to time on various shoots. Never a friend of the captain's. He was sure Bartlett was going to try to cheat over this bet they had. He was very hung over when I saw him on the morning of the murder, but he could have been putting that on for my benefit. He had asked me to be at the castle to referee the shooting, but I refused and told him the colonel would probably take it as a personal insult. Still, his very asking me to be there could have been a smoke-screen, for the murder, as we know, took place much earlier.'

'He appears to have told Blair he loathed Bartlett,' said Chalmers. 'The reasons he gave were that Bartlett had pinched his toothbrush and used it to scrub his toes, and evidently the captain had a disgusting habit of shaving in the bath. Makes you wonder what the ladies saw in a man like that.'

'Och, women are funny,' said Hamish. 'Take the case of Heather Macdonald, her that was married to a fisherman. She kept that cottage of theirs so clean, it wasnae human. You had to take off your boots and leave them outside when you went visiting. She wouldn't allow him to smoke and she starched the poor man's shirts so stiff, it was a wonder he could sit down in the boat. But she ups and offs last year wi' a tinker from the side-shows at the Highland games, and he was a dirty gypsy who didn't have a bath from the one year's end to the other. I don't think,' added Hamish sadly, thinking of Priscilla, 'that the ladies are romantic at all.'

Chapter Nine

The wild vicissitudes of taste.
— Samuel Johnson

Priscilla had decided to visit Mrs Mackay, she of the green bottle and the bad leg. Henry had readily agreed to go with her. Putting thirty miles between himself and Tommel Castle seemed an excellent idea.

Despite the police investigation, Henry was in a high good humour. He had received a visit from several members of the local Crofters Commission who had formally asked him if he could still be counted on to hand out the prizes at the fair on the following day. They had been courteous and highly flattering. Henry had been made to feel like a local squire.

As Priscilla drove competently along the Highland roads, he looked out across the glittering windy landscape and thought it might be quite a good idea to buy a castle. There seemed to be castles all over Scotland for sale. It would be wonderful publicity. Somehow, he must manage to get himself a coat of arms. If he sold the film rights of *Duchess Darling*, they could film the whole thing in his castle. He had more than enough money to decorate it in style. Then, after his marriage, he would invite journalists from the Sunday newspaper colour supplements. Yes, a castle was a definite possibility.

Priscilla looked beautiful and happy. Just getting away from the gloomy atmosphere of death was enough to make both of them feel like schoolchildren at the beginning of the holidays.

Henry told her to stop when they were on a deserted stretch of road and then took her in his arms. She was passionate and responsive, and he felt a heady feeling of triumph as his hand slid up under her skirt for the first time. But his searching hand stopped short of its goal. He had a sudden prickling feeling at the back of his neck, a feeling he was being watched.

He released Priscilla and turned around. An elderly man was peering in the car at Henry's side.

'What the hell do you think you're doing?' shouted Henry.

'I wass passing,' said the old man in a quavery voice, 'and I thought to myself, thought I, Those people are having the bad trouble with the steering. I saw you both fumbling away.'

'Mr McPhee,' said Priscilla, who had recognized the old man, 'we were not having trouble with anything at all. Thank you for your concern.'

Mr McPhee smiled. 'It is not any trouble at all, at all. Are you sure it is not your clutch that is wrong?'

'No, not *my* clutch,' said Priscilla, and giggled, and that giggle of hers made Henry even more furious.

'Drive on,' he said.

'I haven't introduced you,' said Priscilla. 'Mr McPhee, this is my fiancé, Henry Withering. Henry, Mr McPhee.'

'Oh, of course, you are that playwright that everyone iss talking about,' said Mr McPhee. 'It iss a grand thing to have a way with the words. I mind my daughter Elsie's youngest boy, David, was a fair hand with the words when he wass at the school.'

'Priscilla, will you drive on or do I have to get out and walk?' snapped Henry.

'Goodbye, Mr McPhee,' said Priscilla politely. 'I am sorry we have to rush. Give my regards to the family.'

'How on earth could you bear to be civil to that dirty old Peeping Tom!' raged Henry, as soon as they had started moving.

'He is *not* a Peeping Tom,' said Priscilla. 'His eyesight is bad. He is very old, but very kind and charming. Furthermore, that grandson of his, David, is now the drama correspondent

153

of the *Glasgow Bulletin*. You ought to be nice to people while you're on the way up, darling. You might meet them on the way down.'

'I'm no longer "on the way up",' said Henry crossly. 'I've already arrived!'

Priscilla drove on in a grim silence until they turned off the road and bumped up a heathery track to the Mackays' little white croft house, which was perched on the side of a hill.

'Now, do be nice,' cautioned Priscilla.

'Of course,' said Henry sulkily, wondering whether to remind Priscilla that a leading London columnist had described him as 'the most charming man in London'.

Henry brightened perceptibly as soon as they were inside the croft house. He was always on the look-out for things to add to his store of witty after-dinner conversation. He took one look around the Mackays' living room and treasured up each bit of bad taste. The carpet was virulent green and ornamented with sugar-pink cabbage roses. The wallpaper was in an orange-and-black abstract pattern. There were horrible china ornaments everywhere: cats, dogs, little girls holding up their skirts. The tea-cosy was a doll in a crinoline gown. There was an enormous china wall-plaque above the fireplace depicting a cottage in shrieking reds and yellows and decorated with a dusting of tinsel, bearing the legend 'My Grannie's Hielan' Home'.

He set himself to please. He described famous people he had met and exotic countries he had been to. He punctuated his conversation with many 'Of-course-this-will-come-as-a-surprise-to- you-buts', until gradually he began to wonder if he had said something wrong.

Priscilla was very still and silent. The Mackays, at first courteous and animated, began to look at him stolidly.

Henry could not bear unpopularity. He began to ask them questions about themselves, which they answered in polite monosyllables.

When Priscilla stood up and said they must leave, it was a relief.

They drove off in silence, and then Priscilla said in a small voice, 'Did you have to be so patronizing, Henry?'

'I behaved very well,' said Henry stiffly. 'Good God, Priscilla, they're not the easiest of people to talk to. They're as thick as pig shit.'

'They are not! They are very intelligent and very sensitive and they knew immediately you thought the things in their house were a hoot. You kept looking round at everything with a sort of unholy glee.'

'You'll be saying next I should admire their taste,' scoffed Henry. 'All those ghastly ornaments. And that carpet screaming at the wallpaper.'

'It's cosy,' said Priscilla. 'Look, if you've been brought up among old, old things that

155

have been used for generations, you have a longing for things that are bright and new. The government grants have made a difference. They have some money for the first time in their lives. It's only people who've been used to comfort who find domestic antiques beautiful. Mr Mackay's son has an arts degree from Glasgow University. These people are *different*. And they often know what you're thinking. What's this big thing about good taste anyway? We went for dinner with those friends of yours before we left London, you know, those two raving queens in Pont Street. Everything was exquisite and the cooking was *cordon bleu*, but they were screeching and vulgar and petty. And in my opinion, anyone who puts funny junk in the loo is the absolute end.'

In the bathroom of Henry's London flat was a framed series of mildly pornographic Victorian photographs.

'Don't preach to me!' said Henry. 'What about the glorious load of fakes in that home of yours? Fake armour, fake panelling – your father's probably a fake colonel.'

Priscilla tightened her lips. If Henry had been a woman, he would have been damned as a bitch, she thought.

'It's no use talking to you,' said Henry. 'Look, this murder has put us all on edge.'

'I am *not* on edge!' Priscilla's angry voice seemed to fill the car. 'You did not have to talk about countries you had been to and then carefully explain where they were on the world map. When you were talking about Lawrence Olivier, you might have called him by his proper name instead of talking about "dear Larry". And I can only assume "darling Maggie" is Princess Margaret, since, in your case, it could hardly have been Margaret Thatcher. I wonder the comrades ever put up with you. They must have loved being patronized. Were you one of those slobs who titillated the left with cosy stories of sodomy and beatings at Eton?'

'Shut up!' shouted Henry, because what Priscilla had said was true.

'No, I won't,' said Priscilla. 'It's almost as if you had unlearned how to be a gentleman, and now you've started being a gentleman again, you've forgotten how to go about it. You even hold your knife and fork as if you're holding a couple of pencils. People like Mr Mackay and yes, even old Mr McPhee, are gentlemen.'

'What do you know about anything, you bloodless little Sloane Ranger?' howled Henry. 'You with your "Not tonight, Henry" and your prissy little disinfected mind.'

'We are definitely *not* suited,' said Priscilla in a quiet voice.

'You're overwrought and talking rubbish,' said Henry in a conciliatory tone. 'Didn't I get on well with those people from the Crofters

157

Commission? Honestly, darling, I am a very popular fellow, or had you forgotten?'

'That's in London,' said Priscilla darkly. 'Everything's different in London.'

Henry shrugged and fell silent. She was in a bad mood. He would talk her round when they got back to the castle.

The day had changed. Great black, ragged clouds were rushing in from the east, a reminder that autumn comes early in the Scottish Highlands. Small wizened trees creaked and swayed beside the road, and the tarns on the moors gleamed black under the looming shadows of the mountains. The Two Sisters, the mountains above Lochdubh, stood up against the sky, as sharply silhouetted as if they had been made out of black cardboard.

Priscilla drove straight past the castle gates, where a group of shivering journalists and cameramen were huddled. She stopped about a mile along the road at a disused lodge.

'It's only a little walk,' she said, 'and it will bring you out in front of the castle.'

'And where are you going?'

'Somewhere,' said Priscilla, tight-lipped.

Henry muttered something under his breath and climbed out.

After Priscilla had roared off, he turned about to walk back to the main gates of the castle. Why should he let the chance of a lot of glorious free publicity slip past? And he had seen a London television unit when they had driven past. When he arrived, the press hailed him with delight.

Hamish was back at the police station in Lochdubh. Detective Chief Superintendent Chalmers was staying at the Lochdubh Hotel. Blair, Anderson, and MacNab had been transferred to a boarding-house at the other end of the waterfront.

He was interrupted during his evening chores by two American tourists whose car battery had gone dead. Hamish jump-started it and then invited the tourists in for tea. They were a pleasant couple from Michigan. Hamish, like most Highlanders, felt more at home with Americans than he did with the English. He chatted away happily for an hour and then sent them on their way, telling them to call at the garage when it opened at nine the following morning, and promising to see them at the crofters' fair.

He had noticed while he was entertaining them that the kitchen floor was sorely in need of a scrub. He changed out of his uniform into his old clothes, got a pail of soapy water and a scrubbing brush, and got to work, fending off Towser, who thought it was some sort of game.

He was aware of being watched, and looked up. The evening was growing dark and he had not yet switched on the electric light in the kitchen, but he recognized the slim figure lurking in the doorway.

'Come in, Priscilla,' he said. 'I've just finished.'

'You'd better put down newspapers, Hamish, until the floor dries,' said Priscilla, 'or Towser will ruin your good work.'

'There's a pile on the chair over there,' said Hamish. 'Pass them over.'

'I'll put them down for you,' said Priscilla, switching on the light.

Hamish looked sharply at her, but she quickly bent her head, her thick hair falling forward to shield her face.

'I was just about to have my supper,' said Hamish. 'I would ask you to join me, but I suppose you'll soon be getting back to the castle for your dinner.'

'I would like to stay,' said Priscilla in an uncharacteristically small voice.

'Aye, well, you'd better go ben to the office and call your parents and tell them where you are or they'll be worried.'

'I don't want to tell them I'm here,' said Priscilla.

'No, well, chust tell them you are going round to the Church of Scotland to discuss the arrangements for the White Elephant stall. We'll go along afterwards and that'll make it all right.'

'All right, Hamish,' said Priscilla meekly. She left the kitchen and he looked curiously after her.

He thought gloomily of the two mutton pies he had bought at the bakery on his road home. Then he shouted, 'I'm stepping out. Back in a minute.'

He ran into his back garden and cleared the fence with one lanky leap. He knocked on his neighbour's door.

Mrs Cunningham, a faded English lady who ran a bed-and-breakfast, answered the back door.

'I hae a guest for supper,' said Hamish breathlessly, 'and I've only got mutton pies and I cannae be offering her those.'

Mrs Cunningham folded her thin arms over her scrawny bosom.

'Constable Macbeth,' she said severely, 'you promised to unstop that drain-pipe of mine.'

'Tomorrow,' said Hamish. 'I'll be round in the morn wi' ma ladder.'

'Promise?'

'Aye, cross ma heart and hope to die.'

'Well, Mrs Wellington, her up at the church, gave me a venison casserole because I promised to help her out, baking the cakes and scones for the fair. I can't stand venison. You can have it.'

'Thanks,' said Hamish.

Soon he was back in his kitchen. The sound of running water came from the bathroom.

Priscilla had decided to wash her face and put on fresh make-up.

Hamish put the casserole in the oven and pulled the cork on a bottle of red Bulgarian wine that one of the fishermen had bought in Ullapool from a member of the Eastern Bloc fishing fleet and had passed on to Hamish.

When Priscilla appeared, he suggested they should go into the living room and have a drink until dinner was ready. Hamish felt that venison casserole merited the title of dinner.

'Have a dram,' he said, producing the bottle he had bought to entertain Anderson.

'Going in for the hard stuff?' asked Priscilla. 'I thought you always drank beer.'

'So I do, but I can tell you this, Priscilla – sometimes there are things that happen that call for a good stiff belt o' the cratur.'

'Yes,' said Priscilla gloomily. 'I'll have a stiff one.'

'Now, what's the matter?' asked Hamish, when they were both seated.

'I don't want to talk about it,' said Priscilla. 'Tell me about the case.'

'We had a rough afternoon,' said Hamish, settling back in his chair. 'Sir Humphrey received us in his bedroom, muttered about two sentences, and fell asleep. Then that Diana was flouncing and bitching all over the place. You didnae tell me she had been engaged to Bartlett.'

'I thought you knew.'

'I know now. But she says she ditched Bartlett, not the other way round. She was seen approaching Bartlett's bedroom on the night of the murder. She said she was on her way down to the kitchens. Screamed she hadn't slept with him, and when we said we knew the brave captain had had Vera, Jessica, and Diana all on the same night, she broke down and yelled that Vera had done it . . . the murder, I mean. Jessica was worse. She said Diana was an expert shot . . .'

'You mean Peter slept with all three of them? That man is disgusting.'

'Maybe. Maybe the ladies are chust as disgusting. Then came the Helmsdales. We couldn't separate them. Bartlett had nearly burnt down their home and Helmsdale had tried to shoot him and Lady Helmsdale had broken his jaw. When taxed with it, they told us we were lying. We couldnae get a bit o' sense out the pair of them. It was like trying to get a statement from Tweedledum and Tweedledee.'

'Don't you think it might have been someone outside the castle?'

'It could well be, but something in my bones tells me it's one of them up at Tommel. Where did you go today?'

'Henry and I went to call on the Mackays.'

'How's her leg?'

'It's better. But she needs an operation on her varicose veins.'

'If she needs an operation, why is Brodie giving her medicine?'

'Because he knows and she knows what the matter is. But she's frightened of hospitals and she belongs to the old school and expects the doctor to give her some medicine when he calls. I shouldn't think there's much in her green bottle of medicine but coloured water.'

'Aye, he's terrible against the pills and bottles, is Dr Brodie. I was surprised he gave Sir Humphrey tranquillizers.'

'Probably nothing more than Milk of Magnesia. He says if people think they're getting tranquillizers' they calm down amazingly.'

'Captain Bartlett once broke a valuable piece of china at Sir Humphrey's.'

'That was terrible,' said Priscilla. 'He's a fanatical collector.'

They drank more whisky and then moved through to the kitchen for dinner. The venison casserole was excellent, and Hamish accepted Priscilla's compliments on his cooking without a blush. They giggled over the nastiness of the Bulgarian wine, and then, after supper, went along to the Church of Scotland manse.

Priscilla had drunk so much, she was a little unsteady on her feet, and Hamish took her arm. The sky had cleared, the weather making another of its mercurial changes. The cold wind had dropped, although angry little waves smacked against the shingle of the beach.

'I had two American tourists in for tea,' said Hamish.

'That'll be the Goldfingers from Michigan,' said Priscilla. 'They're staying at the Lochdubh Hotel.'

'And how did you learn that?'

'I saw Jessie in the village when I was coming to see you. She told me all about them. She was on her way to see if she could catch a glimpse of them.'

'But why? There's nothing odd about them.'

'It's the name, silly. She thinks they're out of a James Bond movie.'

Priscilla reached the manse just in time. She had only been in the door two minutes before the phone rang and it was her father, his voice sharp with anxiety, demanding to know when she would be home.

'I won't be much longer, Daddy,' said Priscilla.

'Well, leave your car at the police station and get that useless copper, Macbeth, to run you back. I don't like the idea of you being out on your own with a murderer on the loose.'

'So you've decided at last it *was* murder,' said Priscilla.

'Never mind what I've decided,' grumbled her father. 'I'll expect you here in half an hour.'

Priscilla was glad of an excuse to cut short her visit, for she did not like Mrs Wellington, the minister's wife, a bossy, tweedy woman who bullied her husband.

When they took their leave, Priscilla told Hamish he was expected to drive her home.

'I would have done that anyway,' said Hamish seriously. 'And I want you to lock your bedroom door.'

Priscilla shivered.

'It's funny,' mused Hamish, as they drove up the winding hill that led to the castle, 'Captain Bartlett had a word wi' me when I left the party. He was outside on the drive. He had a premonition something was about to happen to him. There was something took place at that party to give him the feeling he was in danger.'

'I wish it were all over,' sighed Priscilla.

'Henry will look after you,' said Hamish, flashing her a quick sideways look.

'Yes,' said Priscilla with a brittle laugh. 'Aren't I lucky?'

Hamish drove up through the side road to the castle, although he was sure the gentlemen of the press would have packed it in for the night.

He pulled up outside the looming dark bulk of the castle, got out, and held open the door for Priscilla.

'Are you coming in?' she asked.

Hamish shook his head.

'I enjoyed this evening,' said Hamish politely. 'It is a pity you are engaged, for I had it in mind to try that new hotel up the Crask road tomorrow night.'

'The Laughing Trout? I haven't heard very good reports of it, Hamish, but it's only been open a few weeks. Do you mean you thought of taking me there for dinner?'

'Yes. I aye hae a wee bit o' a celebration after the crofters' fair.'

Priscilla turned and looked at the castle. Henry would be wondering what had happened to her. Tomorrow would be a long day. The press would turn up at the fair, and Henry would expect her to pose for photographs.

'It seems a bit odd, but we're old friends, Hamish, and, yes, I would like to go for dinner with you.'

'I am most honoured,' said Hamish courteously. As she turned away, he added sharply, 'Be careful, Priscilla.'

She gave a choked little sob and flung herself into his arms.

He patted her clumsily on the back, murmuring, 'There, there. It iss all right. Hamish will look after you.'

She finally drew back and dried her eyes. 'Sorry, Hamish,' she mumbled. 'See you tomorrow.'

Hamish watched until she had gone inside the castle. He drove sedately to the gates and out on to the road. Then he turned on the police siren full blast and raced down to Lochdubh.

'That policeman's drunk,' said Mrs Cunningham, peeping through her lace curtains.

Two of her boarders joined her at her window. 'Did you ever?' said Mrs Cunningham. 'Blasting that police siren when there's no need at all and now he's doing cartwheels up the side of the house to his back door.'

Chapter Ten

*A crofter's son once defined a croft as a
small area of land entirely surrounded by
regulations.*

– Katharine Stewart

Summer returned for the day of the crofters'
fair. Hamish rose early and unstopped Mrs
Cunningham's drainpipe. He was interrupted
by the superintendent, demanding to know
why PC Macbeth had been sounding his police
siren. Hamish said he had been testing it out,
as he did periodically, because you never
knew when it would come in handy, to which
Chalmers replied, 'Well, go easy on the
booze, son.'

As all the members of the house party were
to attend the crofters' fair, Chalmers said he
had got Colonel Halburton-Smythe to agree to
a further search of all the rooms in the castle.
He ordered Hamish to attend the fair and to
see if he could elicit any further information
from the guests.

Hamish tactfully did not point out that he had promised to attend anyway and that the police car was being used to transport cakes and scones to the fair.

The school kitchens were being used for last-minute baking. When Hamish arrived there shortly after nine o'clock, it was to find all the members of the house party helping out. Even old Sir Humphrey Throgmorton appeared to be completely recovered and was beating batter in a bowl with a gingham apron tied round his waist.

Lady Helmsdale advanced on Hamish with a bowlful of raisin-spotted batter. 'Be a good man,' she boomed, 'and give that a stir while I get on with something else.'

'I'm surprised to see you all here so early,' said Hamish. 'I thought you wouldn't turn up until this afternoon.'

'Got to keep these people on the move,' said Lady Helmsdale. 'Can't have them moping around the castle being badgered by those scribe-chappies and nosy coppers and dosing themselves with tranquillizers. Tranquillizers, pah! Lot of muck, if you ask me. In my mother's day, a good dose of castor oil put an end to stupid fancies. People are getting murdered every day. Can't take this one too seriously. Fact is, the world's a better place without that cad.'

'You cannae expect me to approve of people

170

taking the law into their own hands,' said Hamish.

'Why not?'

'That's anarchy.'

'Nonsense. Bartlett was a cockroach. Someone stepped on him. Jolly good for someone, is all I can say.'

She moved off to make sure everyone was working.

Hamish noticed Priscilla and Henry were working together at a table over in the corner. They seemed to be enjoying themselves. Hamish thought they might have had some sort of reconciliation after a quarrel. They were being playful and giggling a lot, rather like a couple trying to show the world how really happy they were, reflected Hamish, feeling sour with jealousy.

Carrying the bowl, he moved over to join Diana and Jessica.

'Can't we ever get away from the police?' said Diana nastily.

'I'm not policing at the moment,' said Hamish mildly. 'I'm beating cake mixture.'

'I don't mind you joining us,' said Jessica. 'Unlike Diana, I don't have a guilty conscience.'

'I'm tired of your bitching, Jessica,' said Diana. 'Some friend you've turned out to be. You're so jealous of me, you can't resist making a crack at every opportunity.'

'Why on earth should I be jealous of you?' demanded Jessica.

Diana ticked off the items on her fingers. 'I have looks, and you don't. I attract men, and you don't. Peter was wild about me and he thought you were a joke. He said it was rather like screwing the old grey mare who ain't what she used to be.'

Jessica picked up a bowl of batter and slammed it full into Diana's face.

'Now, now,' bleated the Reverend Tobias Wellington, bustling forward. 'Christian charity, girls! Christian charity!'

'Oh, piss off, you old fruit,' said Diana, clawing batter from her face.

Mrs Wellington brushed her husband aside and strong-armed both the girls out of the kitchen into the schoolyard where her voice could subsequently be heard berating both with magnificent force and energy.

'I do wish she wouldn't go on and on,' said Pruney Smythe, appearing at Hamish's elbow. 'It reminds me of my schooldays.'

'Serves them both right,' said Vera Forbes-Grant, with her mouth full of freshly baked cake. 'This stuff's delicious.'

'Leave some of it for the fair,' said Lady Helmsdale. 'You've eaten half a chocolate sponge cake already.'

Diana and Jessica came back, looking chastened. Now that they were both under attack, their odd friendship had resurfaced.

'Ghastly old trout,' muttered Diana. 'I bet she wears tweed knickers.'

'I've a good mind to put a dose of rat poison in her bloody cake,' said Jessica. 'Let's clear off and find a pub. Thank God, they don't have licensing hours in Scotland.'

'Exit Goneril and Regan,' murmured Sir Humphrey.

'Goodness, did someone say something about gonorrhea?' asked Lady Helmsdale.

Sir Humphrey flushed. 'No, no, dear lady. I was referring to the daughters in *King Lear*. Shakespeare, you know.'

'Oh, *him*!' sniffed Lady Helmsdale. 'Can't stand the man. Awful bore.'

With the absence of Diana and Jessica, the cooking party became very merry. Even Freddy Forbes-Grant, who had been mooning around his wife, suddenly brightened up and began to help with the preparations. Jeremy Pomfret, who had been in the grip of an almost perpetual hangover since the murder, drank a glass of Alka Seltzer and began to look almost human again.

Hamish waited around even after the first batch of cakes was ready, hoping Priscilla would look at him or smile at him, or show in some way she had not forgotten their dinner date. But Mrs Wellington sharply ordered him to get a move on, and so he set out with the police car loaded up with boxes of cakes, pies, and scones for the fair, which was to be held on a sloping field at the back of the village.

Colonel Halburton-Smythe and his wife had gone on ahead and were already there, loading up a mass of junk on to a table that constituted the White Elephant stand. It was a sort of recycling of junk. People bought it one year and then handed it back the next. Fat little ponies cropped the grass, their tiny owners strutting about, brandishing large riding crops.

Some gypsies were setting up side-shows. Hamish wandered over. 'I'll be keeping an eye on you lot,' he said. 'No bent rifle sights this year, no glued-down coconuts, and no brick-hard dartboards which no dart could possibly stick in.'

'We've got to make a living,' whined one.

'But you've begun to cheat all the time,' complained Hamish. 'It fair breaks my heart to see the children wasting their pocket money and not even winning a goldfish for their pains.' He picked up a rifle from the rifle range and held it up to his eye. 'Deary me,' he said mildly. 'Bent again. Fix those sights, or get out.'

He wandered off, followed by a volley of Romany curses.

On the other side of the field, Mrs Mackay was setting up her spinning wheel, preparatory to giving her annual demonstration. 'This is the last time ever, Hamish,' she said. 'I feel such an old phoney, me that buys all my clothes from Marks and Spencer.'

'Aye, well, the tourists like it,' said Hamish. 'How's your leg?'

'Better. As long as I don't walk about too much, I'll be all right.'

'I hear you had the royal visit?'

'Oh, Miss Halburton-Smythe and her fellow. Aye. Talk the hind leg off a donkey, he would.'

'I'd better be getting back for the next load,' said Hamish. 'There's the stuff to collect from St Mary's after I've done with the Church of Scotland.'

Like most Highland fairs, the crofters' one dithered along in a chaotic mess until two in the afternoon, when everything suddenly took shape. Henry Withering was right there in the swing of things, buying a sheepskin rug, a Fair Isle sweater, and a bottle opener with a deer-horn handle.

The sun was high in a cloudless sky, and the field where the fair was being held commanded a good view of the loch. The village of Lochdubh looked down at its mirrored reflection. Surprised and delighted children were winning prizes at the fairground stands. The cakes, scones and home-made jam were disappearing fast.

Priscilla had spoken courteously to the press about the murder, about her forthcoming marriage, about her ideas on modern womanhood. Hamish thought she was doing very well. She was wearing a simple blue cotton shirt-waister and she looked cool and fresh.

Hamish did not know that Priscilla was hating every moment of it. The morning had started well with all the fun in the school kitchen. She had promised to be nice to the press for Henry's sake, but after she had given several very lengthy interviews, she told Henry she had talked enough. Taking her arm, he silently piloted her straight into another press interview, this time with a raddled female columnist who smelled of whisky and whose perpetually angry eyes were always on the look-out for another victim to tear to pieces. Normally, she specialized in savagely criticizing Princess Diana's clothes or Prince Charles's speeches, that ruse of the inferior woman journalist who tries to put herself on a par with the famous by putting them down.

Between interviews, Henry had found time to tell Priscilla of his dream of buying a castle and entertaining all the trendy Chelsea set, along with magazine writers and journalists from the Sunday colour supplements. Priscilla felt a lump rising in her throat. Life was beginning to stretch out in front of her in a series of exhausting press interviews. Henry found the Lochdubh community funny and quaint, something to exhibit to his London friends. Priscilla looked around the pleasant, old-fashioned scene, the purple mountains, the tranquil loch, the friendly, innocent faces of the crofters and felt Henry was turning her into a stranger in her own community.

But when it came to the prize-giving, Henry was superb. He made a warm, funny, amusing speech. He presented the first prize – pony racing – to a small child in jodhpurs. He picked her up in his arms and beamed at the cameras. 'He's going to kiss her,' thought Priscilla wildly, and Henry did.

He presented the prize for the best home-made jam and insisted on tasting it, rolling his eyes ecstatically. The crofters were delighted with him. They appreciated hard work, and Henry *was* working hard to make every prize recipient feel special.

'I suppose our date is off,' said a gloomy voice in Priscilla's ear.

She swung about and looked up into the hazel eyes of PC Macbeth.

'Why?'

Hamish shuffled his feet. 'Well, the pair of you seem to be doing just grand. And it now seems odd to have asked out another man's girl.'

'Yes,' said Priscilla bleakly.

'I thought you would be up there with him.'

'I felt I'd had enough exposure to the press for one day,' said Priscilla 'And it's Henry's show.'

'It is that,' said Hamish admiringly. 'If his plays ever flop again, he'd make his fortune as an actor.'

'I doubt it,' said Priscilla. 'Ham actors are out of fashion.' She blushed hotly. 'I didn't mean that. It's the heat.'

'So we are not going out for dinner?'

'I think I could still manage to go,' said Priscilla, not looking at him. 'I mean, it's not as if I can drop in on you any more once I am married. I'll make some excuse and meet you at the police station at seven.'

Hamish looked over her head, his eyes sharpening. The crowd were laughing at one of Henry's jokes. At the back of the crowd loomed the bowler-hatted head of Detective Chief Superintendent Chalmers. Behind him came Blair, Anderson, MacNab, and six uniformed officers.

'Something's up,' said Hamish.

Chalmers and the rest shouldered their way through the crowd to where Freddy Forbes-Grant was standing.

'Excuse me,' muttered Hamish, making off in the same direction. He arrived in time to hear Chalmers saying softly, 'We would like you to come with us, Mr Forbes-Grant.'

'What?' demanded Freddy, turning red with anger. 'Push off. You're spoiling the fun.'

'We do not want to make a public scene,' said Chalmers. 'Think of your wife.'

'What *is* all this?' demanded Vera.

A silence had fallen on the crowd. Henry's voice from the platform tailed off. Old Mr Lewis, who had won the prize for the best marrow, stood with the huge vegetable in his arms and stared open-mouthed.

'Come along,' said Chalmers, taking Freddy by the arm.

'Keep your hands to yourself,' shouted Freddy, jerking his arm free.

Chalmers sighed. 'You leave me no alternative. Frederick Forbes-Grant, I hereby charge you with the wilful murder of Captain Peter Bartlett and would like to caution you that anything you say may be taken down and used in evidence against you.'

'You're mad,' said Freddy, tugging at his handlebar moustache.

A great silence had fallen on the crowd.

Then Vera whispered, 'Oh, no. Look, there's something I've got to tell you . . .'

'Oh, what's the use. I did it,' said Freddy loudly. 'Put on the manacles.'

'Just come along quietly,' said Chalmers.

The police crowded around Freddy and they all began to move away towards the cars.

Hamish caught up with Chalmers. 'Are you sure?' he asked.

'Pretty sure. A pair of thick gloves was found stuffed down the side of a chair in his bedroom. We can't say anything definite until the lab has a look at them, but it certainly appears as if they've been used in the murder. There's a smear of oil on them.'

'But the rooms were searched thoroughly by Blair!'

'Oh, Blair.' The superintendent shrugged.

'He may not be all that bright,' said Hamish, 'but I'm sure when it comes to routine police work, he's pretty thorough.'

'Meaning someone else put them there? But Mr Forbes-Grant has just admitted to the murder.'

'Aye.' Hamish pushed back his cap and scratched his head. 'Do you want me to come along?'

'I don't think there's any need. You stick to your duties here. I'll telephone you when we get a statement and let you know what he said.'

Vera Forbes-Grant was being ushered into a car behind the one that was taking her husband to Strathbane. She looked shocked and excited at the same time.

A buzz of voices rose as the police cars drove away. The press were tumbling out of the beer tent, the less experienced rushing for their cars, the older hacks staying to collect eyewitness accounts of the arrest.

Henry's voice, coming over the loudspeaker system, startled them all. 'I think, for the sake of all the people of Lochdubh who have worked to make this fair a success,' he said, 'we should go on and not let this terrible murder spoil our day. There is nothing we can do. Now Mr Lewis will bring that splendid marrow of his back up to the platform, he will receive his prize. Now, Mr Lewis, tell the folks how you managed to achieve this giant.'

'What happened?' Priscilla found Jessica and Diana standing beside her.

'We've just arrived,' said Jessica, 'and someone said someone has been arrested.'

'Freddy,' said Priscilla. 'They've arrested Freddy for the murder.'

Both girls exchanged startled glances. Then Jessica let out a slow breath of relief. 'Of course, it must have been him,' she said. 'He must have found out about Vera and Peter. That old bag, Vera, will be swanning all over the place now, saying Freddy killed for her sake.'

'I am very sorry for Vera,' said Priscilla. 'It came as a terrible shock.'

'She'll get over it.' Diana shrugged. 'She'll be drooping around the castle by tonight, trying to queen it over the rest of us as if she's some sort of *femme fatale*, instead of the worn-out old trollop she really is.'

'The pair of you make me sick,' said Priscilla, shaken out of her normal calm. 'If Mummy doesn't tell you to pack and leave, then I shall.'

'Don't get so uppity,' said Diana, with a drunken giggle. 'We weren't going to stay anyway. That dump of a castle is enough to make anyone commit murder. Come on, Jessica. Let's have a beer.'

They ambled off, arm in arm.

Priscilla began to feel the beginnings of a headache behind her eyes. The whole scene took on an air of unreality. Flags and striped awnings fluttered in the bright sunshine, the music from the carousel blared out, almost drowning Henry's voice. Henry. That was the only bright spot in this horrible day, thought Priscilla, with a sudden rush of affection for her fiancé. Although he looked as shocked and strained as the rest of them, he was manfully standing out in the glare of the sun, taking time over each presentation, compèring the Highland dancing, accepting the judges' reports for the piping competition, and making the children laugh by pretending a set of bagpipes had come to life and was trying to strangle him.

I'll tell Hamish I can't make it tonight, thought Priscilla, and looked about for the tall figure of the policeman. But there was no sign of Hamish Macbeth.

Hamish was sitting in the beer tent with Diana and Jessica. They had already told him that they had both known all along it was Freddy, although, said Diana, 'At one time I thought it might be Priscilla.'

'Now why on earth would Miss Halburton-Smythe want to murder Captain Bartlett?' asked Hamish.

'There's always been something creepy about Priscilla,' said Diana. 'These repressed virgins can be dangerous.'

182

'How do you know she's a virgin?' asked Hamish curiously.

'You can always tell,' hiccupped Jessica. 'That frozen touch-me-not look always gives them away.'

'And is there something so terrible in being a virgin in your early twenties?'

'It's weird, that's what it is,' said Diana. 'I think Henry's waking up to the fact she's a cold fish. Anytime he calls at her bedroom door, she keeps him standing outside.'

'You're getting away from the murder,' said Hamish.

'No, I'm not. I've seen Priscilla out on the moors with a gun and she handles it like a man.'

'She's all right,' said Hamish, 'but by no means an expert.'

'Known her a long time?' asked Diana slyly.

'Yes.'

'And you're sweet on her,' teased Jessica.

'Aye, I am that, me and the rest of the folk in Lochdubh. We haff always known Miss Halburton-Smythe to be decent and kind, qualities that are as admired in the Highlands as they are anywhere else. It makes a nice change when you think of the silly bitches you sometimes find yourself stuck with. Good day to you, ladies.'

'What's got into him?' asked Jessica, staring after his retreating back.

'Who cares? We'd better put our heads together and find some way to bring Vera down a peg. It's not as if she ever cared a rap for old Freddy . . .'

Hamish walked out of the beer tent. He had a sudden feeling as he made his way through the crowd that Priscilla was looking for him to cancel their dinner date. He did not look round but hurried as fast as he could to his car. Perhaps if he avoided her, she might change her mind.

Jeremy Pomfret was leaning up against his Volvo in the car park. He was smoking a cigarette and beaming drunkenly about him. He hailed Hamish like an old friend.

'Tremendous news about Freddy, hey?'

'I seem to be the only person who's sorry for the man,' said Hamish. 'Why are you so delighted, Mr Pomfret?'

'It's all been hanging over us. I mean, I always knew it must have been one of us. Blair thought I was the prime suspect because of the bet. It's great to know we can all go home now and forget about it.'

'I don't think he did it,' said Hamish abruptly.

'Here, you can't go around saying things like that!' exclaimed Jeremy, turning pale. 'The police said he did it, Freddy said he did it, so it's all wrapped up nice and tight.'

'In my opinion,' said Hamish, 'the murderer's still on the loose.'

'You'd better be careful,' said Jeremy. 'You'd better be very careful, Macbeth. Halburton-Smythe don't like you. He's already had Blair in trouble with the Chief Constable. Blair's a detective. He can stand a bit of aggro. But you're nothing but the village bobby.' Jeremy's normally pleasant expression had changed to one of dislike and suspicion.

Hamish touched his cap and turned away.

'Keep out of it,' Jeremy shouted after him. 'Just keep out of it! D'you hear?'

Hamish got in his car and drove down to the police station. Priscilla's car was still parked outside. Her parents must have run her down to the village in the morning.

He went into his office, sat down at his desk, and called police headquarters at Strathbane. He was told Chalmers was busy and could not come to the phone.

Hamish sighed and took out his notebook, where he had jotted down odd fragments of information about the house guests. He read them over and over again, and then put his large regulation boots up on the desk and thought hard.

The sharp ringing of the phone a half-hour later startled him. He snatched it, expecting the call to be from Chalmers, but it was only Mrs Wellington, the minister's wife, demanding his help in carrying tables and chairs back to the church hall.

Hamish was just leaving when the phone rang again. But before he picked it up, he had a feeling that the caller was Priscilla, still trying to cancel the dinner date.

He put on his cap and left the police station, leaving the phone ringing.

'Where have you been?' asked Henry Withering as Priscilla walked up to him.

'I've just been to the phone box down the road to call someone in the village,' said Priscilla. 'It's someone I promised to visit this evening and I wanted to tell . . . her I couldn't make it.'

'I should think not,' said Henry with a grin. 'You've got me to look after.'

'You don't seem to need much looking after,' said Priscilla. 'You've been marvellous today, Henry. The fair would have been a disaster without you.'

'I think I've done enough,' said Henry. 'Let's get back to the castle and have a nice cool drink. Where's your car?'

'It's down in the village, but anyone in the car park will give us a lift.'

'Okay, I'll just say my goodbyes to the Crofters Commission people and join you in a minute.'

Priscilla waited until he had gone and then took a notebook out of her handbag and scribbled a message to Hamish on a sheet of paper. She could pop it through the letter box of the police station when she got there. She finished the note and looked for Henry. He was talking earnestly to her father about something. Colonel Halburton-Smythe laughed and clapped him on the shoulder.

Daddy's so pleased with him, thought Priscilla. I *have* done the right thing.

Henry and Priscilla were dropped outside the police station by Mrs Wellington. They had passed Hamish on the road. Mrs Wellington had signalled to him to stop, but the policeman had either not seen her, or had pretended not to.

'What on earth is your car doing at the police station?' demanded Henry.

'Didn't I tell you?' said Priscilla. 'Daddy phoned when I was calling on Mrs Wellington last night and told me to get Hamish to run me home.'

'I thought he didn't like him.'

'He doesn't. But Daddy was concerned about my safety. I just have to leave a note for Hamish about some church arrangements.' She pushed open the garden gate of the police station and Towser treated her to a slavering welcome.

'Don't be long, darling,' called Henry. 'I need that drink before the press conference.'

Priscilla turned back and leaned on the garden gate. 'What press conference?'

'This is big news. They'll all be back at the

castle tonight. I've got your father to agree to let me hold a press conference and deal with the media for him.'

'But Daddy's way of dealing with the media is to lock them outside the estate,' said Priscilla, 'and a bloody good idea, too. I've talked and talked and talked today on your behalf, Henry. I've had cameras poked in my face and I've had to parry some pretty personal questions. There's been an arrest. Vera's going to be in need of some looking after.'

'Oh, Vera.' Henry shrugged. 'That one will be enjoying every minute of the drama.'

'Vera's all right,' said Priscilla. 'For all her nonsense, she really does care for Freddy. Can't you keep the press away?'

'Until I see a contract for the film rights and make sure a secondary company has taken *Duchess Darling* on the road, I won't feel secure,' said Henry. 'Okay, I know this murder's dreadful. But it's a windfall for me. No publicity is bad publicity, and you'd better get used to that. So just deliver that note and let's get going.'

Priscilla looked at the note in her hand. She walked up to the front of the police station. She stared at the letter box. Then she raised the flap and let it bang and walked back to the car with the note still crumpled up in her hand.

'Ready to go?' said Henry.

'Yes, ready,' said Priscilla evenly.

* * *

Hamish returned to the police station at six. He switched on his answering machine. A Gaelic voice wailed out the beauties of Lochnagar. He switched it off. He must really find out how it worked one day.

He phoned Strathbane again and this time got through to Chalmers.

'He's given us a full confession,' said Chalmers. 'Seems quite cocky about it all now. Says he knew Bartlett had had an affair with Vera and so bumped him off. The lab's still working on the gloves. They were the ones used in the murder, all right.'

'But can't they tell from the swabs they originally took from Freddy's hands and the inside of the gloves whether he actually wore them?'

'Don't know. One of the boffins has come up with a theory that Freddy actually used fine surgical gloves under the heavy leather ones.'

'And what does Mr Forbes-Grant say to that?'

'Says he can't remember. Says we've got our murderer, so why are we wasting time with a lot of damn-fool questions.'

'And Vera Forbes-Grant – she was about to tell you something at the fair. What was it?' asked Hamish.

'She says she just wanted to tell us that her husband couldn't have harmed anyone. But she seems to have changed her tune. She's actually *proud* of him. Can you credit that?'

'Aye, in a way,' said Hamish cautiously. 'I'm no' easy in my mind about this. I cannae think Freddy would have been cold-blooded enough. The murder may have been done on the spur of the moment, but it was done by someone who didn't lose his head and thought of everything. I don't like those gloves turning up conveniently like that.'

'I'm under a lot of pressure,' said Chalmers. 'I *want* the murderer to be Forbes-Grant. I want the Chief Constable off my back. I want the press off my back. What's up with the news these days? Why don't the Libyans bomb Harrods or something? Why doesn't another Russian reactor blow up?'

'Now, now,' said Hamish soothingly. 'It is of no use wishing a section of the population to die a terrible death just to get the press off your back.'

'Everyone will be on my back tomorrow,' sighed Chalmers. 'I'm going back to that castle and I'm going to take them all through their statements again, and I'm going to have as many men as can be spared combing the moors for more clues.'

'Have you told the colonel yet?'

'That's my next call,' said Chalmers gloomily. 'I'll expect you at Tommel Castle at nine in the morning. Where will you be if anything crops up?'

'The Laughing Trout.'

'Dear God.'

'It's a new restaurant, up on the Crask road.'

'Personally, I wouldn't go near any place with a twee name like that. Enjoy yourself.'

Chalmers rang off.

Hamish rushed to wash and change. It looked as if Priscilla was going to keep the date after all.

Chapter Eleven

I maintain that though you would often in the fifteenth century have heard the snobbish Roman say, in a would-be off-hand tone, 'I am dining with the Borgias tonight', no Roman ever was able to say, 'I dined last night with the Borgias'.
— Max Beerbohm

'No, Hamish,' said Priscilla Halburton-Smythe severely. 'You cannot keep Uncle Harry's clothes.'

Hamish stood sheepishly in front of her in all the splendour of Uncle Harry's dinner jacket and trousers.

'I'll take them off,' he said. 'You are only wearing a sweater and trousers, so I'll look a bit odd.'

'Keep it on for the evening,' said Priscilla. 'I've got a dress and high heels in this plastic bag. I had to climb out the back way.'

'I suppose the press were all there,' said Hamish sympathetically.

'They were all inside, being entertained by Henry. He felt it would be better to get it all over with rather than being pestered by them when we tried to go out of the castle gates. But I'm afraid I couldn't face them myself. You know how it is. Mummy would never even begin to understand why I wanted to go out for dinner, so I climbed out of the window of that little upstairs drawing room that nobody ever uses and slid down the roof. No one saw me leave, not even the servants. I'd left my car down the side road.'

'Won't Henry be upset when he finds you missing?'

'He won't. I'll climb back in the way I climbed out. I told him I was going to bed and I locked my door on the inside when I left. I'll only be a minute changing.'

She disappeared into the bathroom and Hamish sat down to wait. This must be what it's like when you have an affair with a married woman, he thought. I wish Henry didn't exist. I wish we could go out for an evening without all this secrecy.

Priscilla emerged in record time wearing a filmy red chiffon dress and high-heeled black patent leather sandals.

'You'd better hide your car in the garage and we'll take the police car,' said Hamish.

While she put her car away, he locked up the police station and then stood holding open the door of his car for Priscilla. She got in with a flurry of chiffon skirts and black-nyloned leg just as Mrs Wellington walked past.

'Evening,' said Mrs Wellington, her eyes bulging with curiosity.

Hamish slammed the car door before Priscilla could say anything, jumped into the driving seat and drove off with a roar.

'That's torn it,' said Priscilla. 'She'll tell Daddy.'

'He would be bound to hear sooner or later,' said Hamish. 'You cannae keep anything quiet around here.'

'I know that,' said Priscilla. 'I was just hoping it would be later rather than sooner.'

The Laughing Trout, previously called The Caledonian Arms, had reopened under the new name only recently. The first sinister sign of a possibly indifferent kitchen to meet Hamish's eye was a row of painted cartwheels against the fence of the parking area. People who went in for painted cartwheels, reflected Hamish gloomily, often had peculiar ideas about food.

A harassed woman answered the bell in the small reception and told them they were lucky there was a table free, and to go and wait in the bar.

Hamish ushered Priscilla into the bar and they sat down in two mock leather armchairs in front of an electric log fire.

The harassed woman handed them enormous menus and rushed off.

'What would you like to drink?' asked
Hamish.

'Campari and soda.'

'I'll have the same.'

'I've never seen you drink Campari and
soda before,' said Priscilla.

'And never will again,' said Hamish. 'But
I've a feeling that this is the sort of place where
they'll be better able to cope with two of the
same kind of drinks.'

'Do you think they come and serve you, or
do you have to go to the bar?'

'I think I'll need to go and get them,' said
Hamish.

The bearded barman was demonstrating
back casts to a balding gentleman who was
wearing a double-breasted blazer with an
improbable crest.

He ignored Hamish and continued talking.

'I'm telling you, that was a twenty-pounder
at the end of my line, and I knew it,' he was
saying.

An unhealthy-looking girl came into the bar
behind the counter, fiddled with the till, and
went out again.

Hamish sighed. He had come across this
sort of situation before. In some mysterious
way, various cockney families seemed able to
find out when a new hotel was about to open
up and they descended on it *en masse*, offering

their services – uncle behind the bar, mother at reception, daughter and auntie in the kitchen. They ruined the trade with bad manners and worse food before flying off, like locusts, to descend on yet another Highland hotel.

Hamish took a step back. Then, with a flying leap, he vaulted the bar and, ignoring the barman's cries of outrage, proceeded to pour two Campari and sodas.

'I'll call the police,' shrieked the barman.

'I am the police,' said Hamish. 'If you do not behave yourself, I shall take time off and check that gantry to make sure all your measures comply with government regulations.'

'No need for that,' said the barman. 'I didn't see you waiting. You only had to ask.'

'And a fat lot of good that would have done me,' said Hamish. 'Lift the flap, put these on my bill, and shut up.'

He carried the drinks back to Priscilla.

'I've a feeling we should leave,' she said.

'Oh, let's stick it out,' said Hamish. 'Cheers. What's on the menu?'

'Very little, especially when you consider the enormous size of the thing. I'll read it out. First course is a choice of Rabbie Burns Broth, Mary, Queen of Scots Sizzling Scallops and the Laughing Trout's Pheasant Pâté.'

'I'll try the broth.'

'So will I. Next comes Truite à la Flora Macdonald, Poulet Écossais and Gaelic Steak. What on earth is a Gaelic Steak?'

'A herring.'

'Seriously.'

'I havenae the faintest idea.'

'The menu,' said Priscilla, 'has been approved by The Wee Touch O' Scotia Society. Never heard of them.'

A pallid-faced waiter drifted up to them. 'Are yiz ready?' he said.

'What's a Gaelic steak?' asked Hamish.

'It's fillet steak flambéed in whisky.'

Hamish looked across at Priscilla, who nodded. 'Well done,' she said.

'Mine'll be the same,' said Hamish, 'and we'll have two broths to start. Where's the wine list?'

'Back o' the menu,' said the waiter.

Hamish turned over the menu. All the wines were from a place called the Clachan Winery. 'Have you not got any French wine?' asked Hamish.

'No,' said the waiter. ''S all Sco'ish.'

'You from Glasgow?'

'Aye, ah'm working in ma holidays. Ah'm at the Polytechnic.'

'Well, here goes. We'll try a bottle of the fine fruity burgundy of Cromarty.'

''S your funeral,' said the waiter, taking the menus and slouching off.

He poked his head back round the door a moment later to summon them to a dining room that smelled overwhelmingly of new paint. Various diners were sitting about talking about fishing in high, strangulated voices.

A grey mess of soup was put in front of each of them along with two half rolls.

'To take my mind off this,' said Hamish, 'how's Vera Forbes-Grant?'

'She came back just before I left and Mummy was looking after her. She's awfully proud of Freddy. She even was prepared to see the press, but Henry ... Henry thought it would be best if he saw them alone.'

'Chust so,' said Hamish, bending over his soup.

Priscilla flushed. 'It's not as if Henry's *hogging* the press, it's just he thought Vera might say something she shouldn't and that wouldn't help Freddy at his trial.'

'When are you thinking of getting married?'

'I don't know,' said Priscilla miserably. 'I suppose Mummy'll organize all that.'

'Are yiz finished?' asked the waiter at Hamish's elbow.

'Aye,' sighed Hamish, 'you can take mine away.'

'And mine,' said Priscilla.

'Who's going to be the first to taste the wine?' said Hamish.

'I notice he didn't have the courage to let you try it first,' said Priscilla. 'Let's both drink at the same time. A toast! No more murder.'

'No more murder,' echoed Hamish, raising his glass.

199

Priscilla took a sip and wrinkled her nose. 'Tastes a bit like turpentine.'

'I hope the steak's all right. You can't do much to ruin a fillet steak. I'm surprised you like yours well done as well. I thought everyone ate them rare these days.'

'Not any more.'

The waiter placed two plates of steak and vegetables down in front of them.

'Considering the prices they charge,' said Hamish, 'you would think they'd put the vegetables on separate dishes.'

Priscilla sank her knife into her steak. Blood gushed out on to the plate.

'Here, laddie!' called Hamish. The waiter slouched up.

'We said well done,' protested Hamish. 'These are raw.'

'Aye, weel, that's the way a Gaelic steak's cooked.'

'And what way is that supposed to be?'

The waiter drew himself up to his full height of five feet four inches, puffed out his chest, and declaimed, 'It is put in the pan and the whisky is poured over it and then it is flambéed.'

'But it's supposed to be cooked a bit before you set it on fire,' complained Hamish. 'Take it away and cook it properly.'

'But you ordered a Gaelic steak and that's what you got,' said the waiter.

'There is no such thing as a Gaelic steak,' said Hamish, exasperated. 'It is a figment o' your overheated brain.'

Hamish picked up both plates and stalked off to the kitchen.

'Won't do him any good,' said the waiter gloomily.

The barman, the cook, the receptionist, the bookkeeper, and a maid were all sitting round a table in the kitchen eating fish and chips. They all shared a startling family likeness.

Hamish took one look at their pinched cockney faces and headed for the stove. 'Don't ask me what I'm doing,' he said, over his shoulder, 'for if I hear one more word about Gaelic steaks, I might forget myself and tell ye what to do with them.'

'He's the police,' said the barman gloomily. They all stared stolidly as Hamish melted butter in a pan and proceeded to fry the steaks.

'Just go on eating as if he wasn't here,' said the barman.

'What's this?' demanded Hamish suddenly, looking at a rack of good French claret.

'We keep that for special customers,' said the cook.

Hamish finished frying the steaks in grim silence. He put them back on the plates, tucked a bottle of claret under his arm, and made his way back to the dining room.

'It would hae been better to have cooked you a meal back at the police station,' he said to Priscilla. 'It makes me sick the way the Scottish Tourist Board moans on and on about the decline o' tourists. If they checked up on places like this, they might get them to come back.'

'Never mind, Hamish. It tastes lovely now and you've got us some decent wine.'

'I was silly to bring you here,' said Hamish. 'We could have gone to the Lochdubh Hotel. The only reason I didn't want to go there was because your father would have heard all about it before we'd even sat down. I thought if we came here, he might not find out until tomorrow.'

'As it is, it's a wonder he hasn't phoned already,' said Priscilla. 'Mrs Wellington will surely have told him by now.'

'But not where we've gone,' pointed out Hamish.

The other guests had left. They were alone in the dining room.

'Who do you think murdered Bartlett?' asked Hamish after a brief silence. 'You must have thought about it.'

'I didn't really. I was pretty sure it must have been someone from outside. I know Mummy's guests are pretty obnoxious, but . . .'

'Yes, why are they obnoxious? I mean, why ask those particular people?'

'A lot of people were pressing for invitations to meet Henry. Mummy just chose the first and most pressing requests. We owed the Helmsdales and Sir Humphrey hospitality. Pruney's all right. Mummy thought, for some hare-brained reason, that Diana and Jessica were friends of mine. Jeremy had already been invited anyway. It just happened, that's all.'

'What were the Helmsdales like when you stayed with them?'

'I never really thought about it. Their place is comfortable, the food is appalling, and the guests usually entertain themselves. We stayed there for a week last October. I travelled up from London. I've known both of them since I was a child. Lady Helmsdale is always so massive and booming that one never thinks of her as a woman with normal jealousies and weaknesses and that sort of thing. Helmsdale himself is a caricature of the Scottish landed aristocracy. I don't really believe he thinks deeply on any subject.'

'Odd, when you think of it,' said Hamish. 'They, the Helmsdales, I mean, must have been in love at one time.'

'Oh, I shouldn't think so,' said Priscilla, surprised. 'One always marries someone suitable, you know, if one is like them. She was a Tarrison, you know, the big flour company, and he had a title and needed money. That's the way it's done.'

'And what about your case? You wouldn't marry someone just to please your parents?'

'It's not so strange. I mean the whole idea of having a Season is to meet the right sort of bloke.'

'But the Season's finished. You don't get presented to the Queen any more or anything like that.'

'No, the court presentations went out a long time ago. They tried to replace the ritual by having the debs curtsy to a cake at the Grosvenor House Hotel, but that began to seem pretty damned silly after a bit. But it still goes on – quieter, maybe. One's parents throw a cocktail party to tell people one's Out, and then bung one into secretarial college while one lives in squalid digs with a lot of other debs. But one still goes to Ascot, Henley, and Goodwood and all that. The pas and mas are very much in the background but they ferret out who has money and who hasn't, and who's pretending to be one of the upper set, but isn't.'

'Amazing,' said Hamish. 'Here we are, rushing towards the end of the twentieth century, and here am I, a respectable bobby who has to take you out in secret, just as if I were the footman in Victorian times.'

'It's all my fault,' said Priscilla miserably. 'I should stand up for myself. I'm all Daddy and Mummy have got and I can't bear to disappoint them.'

'By going about with someone like me? You're awf'y young, Priscilla.'

'I'm old enough to know my own mind and to know that I should not be creeping around having dinner with you at some tatty restaurant when I'm newly engaged.'

'Yes, why *did* you come out this evening?'

'I forget,' said Priscilla, tears standing out in her eyes.

'I shouldnae be grilling you,' said Hamish gently. 'It's all none o' my business, after all. Did you hear what happened to Peter Fisher, him that went down to Ullapool to see if he could defect to Russia?'

Priscilla shook her head and Hamish leaned back in his chair and proceeded to tell a long and extremely Highland story about the adventures of Peter Fisher until Priscilla began to laugh.

Then he got Priscilla to tell him some of her adventures as a fashion editor's assistant.

It was beginning to get dark outside, and suddenly Hamish became aware that they had been sitting in the deserted dining room for some time.

'I'd better get the bill,' he said regretfully. He crossed to the wall and pressed a bell.

After some time, the waiter appeared, minus his white jacket.

'Ah thocht ye'd be awa' hame tae yer beds,' he said.

'I could hardly do that without paying the bill,' said Hamish.

The waiter jerked his thumb in the direction of the kitchen. 'He says it's on the house.'

'If by "he" you mean the barman who's probably the manager as well, go and tell him from me that I know this place is owned by the Belmont Catering Company, and there is no reason to cheat them further. Get my bill.'

The waiter went off and eventually slouched back with the bill. Hamish noticed he had not been charged for the bottle of claret, but felt he could not bear any more argument. He paid the bill, and when the waiter had left, he looked sadly at Priscilla.

'In a way, this is goodbye, Priscilla,' he said. 'As you say, you will not be able to drop in at the police station when you're a married woman.'

He held out his hand, and Priscilla slipped her own into it. She looked into his eyes, wanting to tell him all her worries about Henry, about the engagement, and yet feeling it would be disloyal to Henry to discuss him with another man.

'Sorry to interrupt,' came a sarcastic voice from the dining room door.

Hamish dropped Priscilla's hand as if it were a hot brick and turned about.

Anderson was standing in the doorway. 'Chalmers sent me to get you,' he said. 'There's been another murder.'

'There *can't* be,' gasped Priscilla. 'Did Freddy escape?'

'It wasn't Freddy,' said Anderson heavily. 'Mr Forbes-Grant's secure in prison in Strathbane. His wife's been murdered.'

'Vera!' cried Priscilla, hanging on to the table. 'How?'

'Poison. Someone poisoned her.'

Chapter Twelve

Thou shalt not kill, but needs not strive
Officiously to keep alive.

                – Arthur Clough

'This gets more like a Hammer horror movie every day,' grumbled Henry Withering.

No one answered him. They were all huddled in the drawing room, listening to the footsteps of the police moving about upstairs in Vera's bedroom.

'How do they know it's poison?' whispered Priscilla in Henry's ear.

'Don't ask me. Suppose you've only got to look at her. The whole thing's awful. There was a body hanging in the room as well.'

'A body!' squeaked Priscilla.

'Not a real one. Someone had made a pretty lifelike dummy and even embellished it with a handlebar moustache and strung it up over Vera's bed.'

Pruney, who had been crying off and on

since Priscilla's return home, started to sob again, an irritating snuffly sound.

'Let's go outside,' said Henry. 'They can fetch us for statements when they need us.'

Outside the castle, a wind was rushing through the rhododendrons that bordered the drive. A small moon sailed high above through black ragged clouds.

'I have to ask you this,' said Henry. 'I know there's been another murder, and we're all shocked and all that . . . but what the hell were you doing dining out with that copper and all dolled up in heels and a party gown?'

'I had to get away,' said Priscilla. 'You don't understand, Henry. I said I would meet Hamish for dinner because he's, well, an old friend and comfortable to be with. I knew it wasn't the thing to do and I was going to cancel the evening, but then you came out with this press conference business, and I couldn't *bear* it. I just wanted to run away. Henry, how *can* you go on forcing me on the press, just to see a few more grainy photos of yourself and me on the front page?'

Henry sighed. 'You're very young, Priscilla,' he said, unconsciously echoing Hamish. How could she know, he wondered, about the long years of wanting to be recognized, of knowing you could write and seeing the fame go to lesser people? She treated his experiences with the Communists with tolerant amusement, as if his interest in them had been some sort of fashionable fad. But they had cared for him and they had believed in his work, thought Henry, with a sudden longing for the old days of cold rehearsals and chipped teacups in draughty halls. He was famous now, but he missed the camaraderie of the experimental theatre groups and the occasional mothering laced with unselfish love from intense young girls who were prepared to die on the barricades to change the world.

He sighed again. Sometimes it was hard to know what *was* the real world. For a moment at the crofters' fair, he had felt sure he had found his niche in life at last. He had felt he belonged. Now, it all seemed as if he had been taking part in some brightly coloured sort of *Brigadoon*.

Instead he said, 'You've got to stop running around with that copper, Priscilla. Do you want to break our engagement?'

'Yes. No. I don't know,' said Priscilla wretchedly. 'Mummy and Daddy were so pleased.'

'Do you mean to say you only got engaged to me because you thought I was suitable? You'll be wearing a crinoline next.'

'I can't explain, Henry,' said Priscilla. 'Right at this moment I don't know what I think. Who on earth killed Vera?'

'She might have done it herself.'

'It doesn't seem possible. She was actually proud of what she thought Freddy had done.'

211

'Meaning you don't think Freddy did it?'

'Well, Hamish doesn't.'

Henry drew a deep breath.

'Until you make up your mind to break the engagement, do me a favour and keep that man's name out of our conversation.'

'It happened quite early on in the evening,' Chalmers was saying to Hamish at that moment as they both stood in Vera's bedroom. The body had been taken off to Strathbane.

'It seems she went up to her room about seven and started screaming the place down. Everyone rushed up. Vera was gabbling and pointing at that dummy strung up over the bed. She rounded on the others and accused them all of playing a nasty trick, ordered them out, and locked herself in. About eight o'clock, that Diana went up to her room and passed Vera's on the way. She said she heard scrabblings and choking noises. Asked why she didn't call for help, she said she just thought Vera was carrying on to get attention.

'The guests and the Halburton-Smythes are now convinced she took her own life. I can't look at it that way. I think we've got the wrong man in prison in Strathbane, and that someone else killed Bartlett and then killed Vera because she knew something.'

'Maybe she did,' said Hamish. 'She liked

money. Maybe she was blackmailing the murderer. What was she eating or drinking?'

'Tea and cakes. There was nothing left on the cake plate but crumbs, and those and the dregs from the teapot have been taken away for analysis.'

'She had a terrible sweet tooth,' said Hamish. 'If anyone wanted to poison some cakes – well, we were all down in the school kitchens baking like mad and passing round bowls of stuff to be beaten and putting trays in the ovens.'

'We'd better get down there and have a look and hope they've left the cleaning up until the morning.'

Hamish and Chalmers hurried out to the police cars. Henry was just coming in with Priscilla. He had an arm about her waist. Priscilla avoided looking at Hamish.

The headmistress of the primary school refused to open her door, claiming they were only masquerading as policemen and she had read about thugs like them.

'It's me, Mrs Mackenzie,' called Hamish. 'Macbeth! Take a look through the letter box.'

The letter box was cautiously poked open. Chalmers flicked a lighter under Hamish's face.

There was a squeak of alarm and the metal flap of the letter box dropped. 'Hamish Macbeth,' came Mrs Mackenzie's shaky voice, 'does not own a dinner jacket.'

'Mrs Wellington's got a spare key,' said Hamish. 'We'll try the manse.'

Mrs Wellington was wearing a voluminous flannel nightgown when she answered the door. Hamish was glad Mr Wellington had found God, because it certainly looked as if he would need to wait until he got to heaven to get his reward. She went back in and emerged wrapped in a large tweed coat, produced the key, and insisted on accompanying them.

One look at the school kitchen was enough to tell both Chalmers and Hamish that they would be lucky if they found one fingerprint. Tables were scrubbed and counters were shining.

Hamish fished in the pocket of Uncle Harry's dinner jacket and took out his notebook, glad he had transferred it into the pocket with his other bits and pieces before he went out for dinner.

He licked the end of his pencil and then began to write in meticulous shorthand as Chalmers asked Mrs Wellington to remember where everyone was standing and what they were doing.

But Mrs Wellington was one of those bossy women to whom the very rapping out of orders is an end in itself. She had barked at people to do various things and then had moved on to bully someone else without waiting to see whether her orders were carried out or not.

Nonetheless, Chalmers persisted with his questions as the night wore on and a rising wind soughed about the schoolhouse with a lost, wailing sound.

When Chalmers had at last finished, Hamish asked, 'Do you mind if we see the cupboards where you keep your cleaning materials and things like that?'

'I am very tired,' said Mrs Wellington, 'and I see no reason . . . oh, very well. They're over here, underneath the sinks.'

Mindful of Uncle Harry's trousers, Hamish took out a clean handkerchief, spread it on the floor, knelt down and poked his red head into the cupboards. Then he suddenly stiffened and appeared to point like a dog.

He eased the handkerchief out from under his knees and draped it over one hand. He reached into the cupboard and brought out a cylindrical cardboard container with the label Buggo. He read the list of ingredients carefully and then opened the lid.

'Empty,' he said. 'This is roach powder. I haff never heard of the cockroaches being in Lochdubh.'

'It was that American lady, Mrs Fitzgerald, who left it,' said Mrs Wellington. 'You remember her, Mr Macbeth, the one who turned up at the Lochdubh Hotel for her holidays two years ago with a suitcaseful of mosquito repellent, disinfectant, flea powder, ant spray – the works. She gave that roach powder to Mrs Mackenzie for the school kitchen.'

'And did she use it?' asked Hamish, sitting back on his heels.

'I don't know. Ask her.'

'You'd better come along with us. She thinks we're muggers pretending to be policemen.'

'What are you getting at?' said Chalmers.

'Mrs Forbes-Grant loved cakes,' said Hamish. 'Everyone knew that. She was eating all she could in the kitchen this morning. Someone may have made a special batch of cakes, just for her, and put something like this roach powder in them. This powder contains, or did contain when the box was full, sodium fluoride. There were cake crumbs found in her room.'

'We'd better get a box and take everything,' said Chalmers heavily, 'disinfectants, cleaners, the lot.'

Mrs Wellington persuaded Mrs Mackenzie to open her door. Mrs Mackenzie blinked at the packet of roach powder.

'I mind that American lady giving it to me,' she said. 'I didnae like to disappoint her by saying we didn't have any roaches. I just put it under the sink with the other stuff.'

'And you never used it?' asked Chalmers.

'No. I did not have any reason to.'

Carrying the box with the contents of the schoolkitchen cupboards, Chalmers and Macbeth made their way back to their cars.

'That murderer must be laughing at us,' said Chalmers bitterly. 'Not content with poisoning Vera Forbes-Grant, he, or she, put that grisly dummy up above the bed first.'

'Och, no, that was done for different reasons.'

'Who did it?'

'I should think that terrible pair, Jessica and Diana. It's funny, when I first saw them I thought they were a typical couple of country girls. Now I think they're silly and vicious. I'm sure they strung up that dummy.'

'Why? The woman had just seen her husband accused of murder.'

'Because Vera had an affair with Bartlett, and they're still jealous of her. Because Vera probably milked the last little bit o' drama out of our accusing her husband.

'Or maybe you'll find we were meant to discover it was them who played the dirty trick on her. That way, we might not suspect them of the murder.'

Priscilla Halburton-Smythe thought the night would never end. One by one they were called into the colonel's study to make their statements, and each person seemed to be gone an hour. By the time it was Priscilla's turn, she was too exhausted to think clearly. She felt she was living in a nightmare where she was doomed to sit in this study, making statements to the police over and over again. Hamish, still in evening dress, was sitting over by the window. He looked elegant and remote. She wished he were wearing his usual scruffy old clothes or worn uniform. He did not look like the Hamish she knew.

At last she was dismissed. Henry was waiting for her at the foot of the stairs.

'How did it go?' he asked sympathetically.

'As usual,' said Priscilla bitterly. 'I'm an old hand at making statements.'

'Well, I've made mine, and dawn is breaking. Let's go to bed.'

Priscilla looked at him warily.

'Look, darling,' he said, 'surely this is not the night to play the prude.'

'Henry, the last thing on my mind at this moment is sex. I don't believe for a moment that Freddy shot Peter. I think the murderer is one of us – or the murderess. The only thing I'm taking to bed tonight is a hot-water bottle.'

'Very well,' he said coldly. 'But it's beginning to appear to me as if there's every possibility of this rubbish going on after marriage. You may be lousy in bed for all I know. In a way, you're asking me to buy the goods before I see them.'

Priscilla clutched hold of the banister. 'Perhaps you're right,' she said wearily. 'But I am still going to my room alone and I am locking the door behind me.' She turned and went up the stairs.

'I suppose if that village bobby comes knocking, you'll open your door, and your legs, soon enough,' he shouted after her.

Priscilla put her head down and ran up the remaining stairs. She collided with the solid bulk of Lady Helmsdale.

'What were you doing in my room?' cried Priscilla.

'I was looking for an aspirin,' said Lady Helmsdale.

Although Priscilla was tall, Lady Helmsdale seemed to loom over her in the darkness of the corridor.

Lady Helmsdale had pale eyes and they were fixed on Priscilla's face in an unnerving stare.

Fear gripped Priscilla. She realized she had never really known Lady Helmsdale. In fact, what did she know of any of the guests, even Henry?

She gave a choked sob, pushed past Lady Helmsdale into her room, and slammed and locked the door.

But although she undressed, got into bed and clutched the hot-water bottle, she could not seem to get warm.

A timid knock at the door made her heart leap into her mouth.

'Who is it?' she called.

'It is I – Pruney.'

'Pruney, I'm exhausted. Is it very important?'

'Yes.'

Priscilla sighed. She climbed out of bed and opened the door.

Pruney stood blinking at her behind her enormous glasses.

'I've got to talk to someone,' she whispered.

'Come in,' said Priscilla. 'I'm too cold to sleep anyway.' She left the door unlocked, hoping Pruney only intended to stay a couple of minutes.

She sat down on the edge of the bed and Pruney sat next to her, twisting a handkerchief in her nervous fingers.

'What is it?' asked Priscilla gently.

'He loved *me*.'

'Who?'

'Captain Bartlett. He loved me,' said Pruney, striking her bosom, which was covered by the embroidered yoke of her old-fashioned nightgown.

'Did he actually say so?' asked Priscilla.

'Not in so many words, but his *actions* ... He was so kind to me at that party, and ... and ... later when I went upstairs, I saw him. He said he was going to talk to Vera. I said, "Won't Freddy object to that?" He laughed and said, "Freddy won't know. I just rap once on the door and walk quickly away. She knows that's the signal to come to my room."'

'But didn't that tell you that Peter was a philanderer?' said Priscilla awkwardly.

'No, no,' said Pruney eagerly. 'He *explained*. He said, "You must think me an awful flirt, but those days are over. I just have to see her on a matter of business. I'm thinking of mending my ways and settling down." And then he raised my hand to his lips and he kissed it,' said Pruney, holding her right hand against her cheek. 'I looked into his eyes and saw a decent love and concern there, and knew I had been instrumental in making him decide to reform. I have had to listen to rubbish from Jessica and Diana, implying they both had affairs with him. It cannot be true. He wouldn't look at *them*. And Vera! That gross, horrible woman. She has a husband . . .'

'Had,' said Priscilla. 'Vera's dead. Remember?'

'And good riddance,' said Pruney with sudden venom. 'She was probably bumped off by one of the servants. She's the sort of woman who has affairs with servants and milkmen and people of that class. Vera was a murderee.'

She clutched Priscilla's arm in a powerful grip. 'Peter loved *me*,' she cried. 'You do believe me, don't you? Someone has *got* to believe me.'

'Is everything all right, Miss Halburton-Smythe?' came a cool voice from the doorway.

Pruney gasped and jumped to her feet.

Hamish Macbeth stood on the threshold.

'I'm just going,' she squeaked, and scurried out past him.

221

Hamish came in and closed the door.

'What was all that about?' he asked.

'Oh, Peter couldn't leave anything in a skirt alone. He kissed her hand and made poor Pruney think he'd fallen for her. Why are you here?'

Hamish sat down on the bed, and then yawned and lay down and stretched out. 'I'm going away,' he said. 'I chust wanted to make sure you were all right. I had a feeling you'd still be awake.'

'Henry might have been in here.'

'So he might,' said Hamish equably. 'But it wasn't Henry's voice I heard.'

'Where are you going?' said Priscilla, lying down beside him and clasping her hands behind her head.

'Chalmers has decided to try a long shot. He's got the address of that aunt of Bartlett's in London and wants me to go and see her.'

'But the police down there could do that, surely?'

'Aye, but he thinks my famous charm might unearth something. We're getting no farther with the case up here, and things are verra serious. Now, Bartlett got engaged to Diana in London, he ditched Jessica in London. There might be something there, or, failing that, this aunt might know of a further connection between Bartlett and the rest of the guests.'

'How long will you be away?'

'I'm going down on the night train. I cannae get a sleeper in the second class and the police don't run to first-class fares. I'll spend the day in London and then come straight back up.'

'I wish you weren't going,' said Priscilla in a small voice. 'I'm beginning to be frightened of everyone, except Mummy and Daddy, and they never were the sort of parents one could talk to, you know. Earlier this evening, Mummy said with tears in her eyes that the only good thing in this whole mess was my engagement to Henry.'

'Well, that is something,' said Hamish, staring at the ceiling.

'But it's all going wrong, Hamish,' wailed Priscilla. 'I think I'm frigid!'

Hamish slid a comforting arm about her shoulders. 'Now, now,' he said, 'I am thinking that a couple o' murders are enough to freeze anyone.'

Priscilla responded with a choked sob. She buried her head on his chest and began to cry.

'There, now,' said Hamish, pulling her into his arms and stroking her hair. 'Once these murders are solved, you'll be able to see things a bit more clearly.'

Hamish had a sudden pang of sympathy for Henry. Priscilla was wearing a short scanty nightdress and was pressing against him for comfort. He realized she had absolutely no idea of the effect she was having on him.

He grimly tried to keep his thoughts on something else as he rocked her like a child and murmured soothing nonsense in her ear.

'I might have guessed,' said Henry Withering, walking into the room and glaring at the couple on the bed. 'Give me back my ring, Priscilla.'

Priscilla started to say something, but Hamish tightened his grip and looked blandly at Henry. Priscilla took off her ring. Hamish took it from her and held it out to Henry, who walked up to the bed and snatched it.

'You'd better think up something to tell your father in the morning,' said Henry, 'because he's going to hear all about this.'

Priscilla struggled free from Hamish's embrace. 'Henry!' she called desperately. But the slamming of the door was the only answer.

'Now, don't start crying again,' said Hamish. 'You wanted out of that engagement. Didn't you?'

Priscilla hung her head. 'But Daddy's going to be furious.'

Hamish swung his long legs off the bed. 'If you don't start thinking for yourself,' he said, 'you're going to end up in another mess. I'm sick to death of hearing what Daddy and Mummy would think. You're a nice girl, Priscilla, but they've kept you ower young for your own good. Take my advice and go and wake your father and give him your version. And make sure you put it plainly enough.

224

Henry had every reason to think the worst. What a frustrated man he must be! You're enough to try the patience of a saint. I am your old friend Hamish. But a village copper has feelings – and eyes – and you're parading about with practically nothing on.'

Priscilla snatched up her dressing gown and wrapped it around her. 'I'm sorry, Hamish,' she mumbled.

'Aye, well, God knows you're safe enough with me. Chust make sure you cover up when there's anyone else around. I'll be back from London as fast as I can. In the meantime, don't trust anyone. If you're that worried, you might try talking to your mother or father as adult to adult and not like a child.'

'Stop patronizing me, Hamish,' said Priscilla.

'You get back from the world the way you treat the world. You treat me like a big brother. What else do you expect?'

'I expect a little sympathy and understanding. You're as bad as Henry.'

'Poor Henry. There are times when I think you need a good slap on the bum to bring you to your senses.'

'Oh, get out,' said Priscilla wearily, 'and take your so-called charm with you.'

Chapter Thirteen

But, Sir, let me tell you, the noblest prospect which a Scotchman ever sees, is the high road that leads him to England!
                    – Samuel Johnson

The crowded train from Inverness to London gave Hamish ample time to reflect on the stoicism of the British. As they chugged their way through the Grampians, the air-conditioning was blasting into the carriage. People rose and put on their coats and sat down again.

Hamish complained to the guard.

'You're the only person that's complaining,' said the guard sourly. 'If I were you, I'd gang doon the train and find a compartment with the heat on.'

'But there's ground frost tonight,' said Hamish plaintively. 'Why is the air-conditioning on?'

'Fur the American tourists.'

'Oh, the Americans, is it?' said Hamish.

'And here's me thinking you maybe had the Laplanders or the Eskimos on board.'

'It's folk like you that make British Rail a failure,' said the guard obscurely, moving away.

Hamish sighed and took down his overnight bag and made his way along the train. He was glad he was not in uniform. The last time he had worn his uniform on the London train, the passengers had treated him like a walking tourist office.

What on earth *did* the American tourists make of all this? thought Hamish, as he eventually settled into a vacant seat farther down the train. No buffet car and eleven hours to make the journey to London.

'Hello!' piped a small voice.

Hamish looked up.

A boy with a pinched white face was sitting opposite him, clutching a comic. Hamish looked about and then looked back at the child.

'Are you travelling on your own?' he asked.

'Naw, I'm with them,' said the boy, jerking his thumb across the aisle where four men were drinking beer and playing poker.

'Which of them's your dad?'

'None of them,' said the boy.

'Uncle, then?'

'Don't know 'em from Adam.'

Hamish surveyed the white little face and the knowing eyes of the child.

'What's your name?'

'Wee Alec. Alec MacQueen.'

'Well, Alec, what are you doing travelling on this train with four men you don't know?'

'It's my maw's idea,' said Alec. 'Man, I'm fair sick of the trains.'

'Oh, they're friends of your mother?'

'Naw.' Alec put his pointed elbows on the table between them and leaned forward. 'It's like this. If you've got a Family Rail card and you take a child along, you get a third knocked off the price o' the fare. Disnae need to be your own child. Anyone's child'll do. So my maw tells one who tells the other that if anyone wants to borrow me, they can. She charges five pounds a head for my services,' said Alec proudly. 'Then when we get to London, they turn me over to some other blokes who are coming back up. Then I pick up another lot at Inverness and come back down, so's I can go back up with them ones what I come down with.'

'Are you on your school holidays?'

'Aye, but it disnae matter one way or the other. If she's got a good fare, my maw takes me off the school.'

'And do you like it?'

'Naw, I hate it,' said Alec. 'I want to be in the school with my friends.'

Hamish looked wildly round the compartment. There were a lot of children on the train. Were they all for hire?

'Would you like me to do something to stop it?' he asked.

'I would like that fine,' said Alec. 'But I don't want my maw to get in trouble with the police.'

Hamish opened his mouth to say he was a policeman, and then thought the better of it.

Nobody seemed to care about education these days. He couldn't remember the last time he had seen a truant officer. He could call on Alec's mother or report her to the Royal Society for the Prevention of Cruelty to Children, but they were surely overloaded with more dramatic cases of child cruelty.

He chatted idly to Alec until the child fell asleep, his narrow head and greasy, lank hair rolling with the motion of the train.

When they arrived in Edinburgh, Hamish left the train and went in search of a phone. He put through a reverse-charge call to Rory Grant on the *Daily Chronicle*, forgetting it was the middle of the night. But he was in luck. Rory was on night shift.

'What do you want, you great Highland berk?' came Rory's voice over the crackling of a bad line.

'I have often wondered how this word "berk" came about,' said Hamish.

'It's rhyming slang. Berkeley Hunt.'

'Tut, tut, that's no' very nice,' said Hamish, shocked.

'Did you put through this expensive long-distance call just to ask me the meaning of rude words?'

'No, I have a wee story for you.'

Hamish told him about Alec, and then finished by saying, 'I would like to do something to help the boy. He is a kind of Scottish *Flying Dutchman*, if you take my meaning.'

'It's a nice human-interest one. Whether they'll send me to meet the train is another thing. I'm out of favour these days. Didn't even get sent up on that murder of yours – or murders, I gather, from the stuff coming over on the tapes. But I tell you what I'll do. I'll phone the story round for you – there's that big Scottish Sunday's got an office in London – and in return I want you to fill me in on some background on the murders.'

'I will do my best,' said Hamish. 'I have an appointment later in the morning. If you can meet the train, maybe we can have breakfast somewhere.'

'I'll try. If not, phone me at home during the day.'

Hamish ran back to the train and found his seat had been taken by a hot and cross-looking woman. Alec was still asleep. Once more, Hamish collected his overnight bag and went in search of a free seat.

The only one to be found was back in the freezing compartment. With a sigh of resignation, he pulled another sweater out of his bag, put it on, and settled down and tried to sleep.

Somewhere after Carlisle, the air-conditioning went off and the heating came on. He arrived in London eyes gritty with sleep and sweating profusely.

As he got off the train, he looked along the platform and smiled in satisfaction. Rory had done his work well. There were five reporters and three photographers clustered around Wee Alec, who was proudly holding forth, although there was no sign of Rory.

Hamish went to the Gents and changed into a clean shirt, shaved with an electric razor, parked his bag in a station locker, and went in search of breakfast.

At ten o'clock, he took the District Line to Chelsea and walked along the Kings Road to Flood Street, where Captain Bartlett's aunt, a Mrs Frobisher, had a house.

The air felt very warm, and a brassy sun was shining through a thin haze of cloud.

Chalmers had promised to phone and warn Mrs Frobisher of his arrival.

The door to Mrs Frobisher's home was opened by a dumpy, suet-faced girl dressed in a black off-the-shoulder T-shirt, black ballet tights, and scuffed shoes.

'Good morning,' said Hamish politely. 'I am Police Constable Hamish Macbeth of Lochdubh, and I am here to speak to Mrs Frobisher.'

'Get lost, pig,' said the girl. The door began to close.

Hamish put his foot in it. 'Now, what is a beautiful creature like yourself doing using such ugly words?' he marvelled.

'She don't want to see you.'

'Miranda!' interrupted a sharp voice. 'Who is it?'

'It's that copper you don't want to see,' the girl roared over her shoulder.

A door in the hallway opened behind her and an elderly lady emerged, leaning on a cane. Her hair was white, and her face criss-crossed with wrinkles.

She peered around Miranda's bulk. 'You don't look like a policeman,' she said doubtfully. 'I received a call from Scotland, saying an officer would call on me and I told whoever it was that I had no wish to see the police again.'

'I can well understand that,' said Hamish. 'I'll try not to take up too much of your time.'

'You seem harmless enough,' said Mrs Frobisher. 'Come in. Bring us some coffee, Miranda.'

The girl sulked off, crashing her fat shoulders off either wall of a narrow passage at the back of the hall.

'Your daughter?' asked Hamish politely.

'Good heavens, no,' said Mrs Frobisher, leading the way into a small sitting room on the ground floor. 'I am much too old to have a daughter of Miranda's age. Miranda is my maid. I got her from an agency. They send me very strange girls. But then, I don't suppose anyone in their right mind wants to be a maid these days. Now, what on earth do you want? I've talked and talked to policemen about Peter. I don't think I can add any more.'

'There's been another development,' said Hamish, and told her about the murder of Vera.

'Gosh,' said Mrs Frobisher, sitting down abruptly. 'What a frightful thing to happen. Are you sure it wasn't suicide? I always thought that woman was unstable.'

'I think she was killed by someone baking cakes for her with roach powder,' said Hamish. 'It's too nasty and complicated a death for suicide.'

'I met her once,' said Mrs Frobisher. 'Peter brought her here. A greedy woman. Greedy for sex, greedy for money. But I think I know who it is who has been committing these murders. It must be Diana Bryce.'

'And why is that?'

Miranda clumped in with a tray with a pot of coffee and cups, thumped it down, and banged her way out.

'I wasn't sure when I heard about the shooting. But poison! I could well see Diana doing that. She threw every kind of fit when Peter broke off the engagement. She followed him to a night-club and made the most awful scene. He told me about it. The poor boy was worried, I could see that.'

'You were fond of your nephew,' said Hamish gently.

Mrs Frobisher's old wrinkled face crumpled like a baby's, and for a moment Hamish thought she was going to cry. But she eased herself to her feet and poured two cups of coffee.

'Yes, very fond,' she said. 'He was not always so wild, so irrational. He was quite bright at Sandhurst, and seemed set for a good military career. He was always taking up hobbies and then dropping them. I always told him he was turning my home into a graveyard for his abandoned hobbies. There's his stamp collection, his model airplanes, his computer, his wood carvings, his . . . oh, so many things.'

'I would like to see them, if I may,' said Hamish.

'His parents died when he was still at school,' said Mrs Frobisher, her eyes staring past Hamish to days of long ago. 'I took care of him. I don't have any children of my own. But after he left Sandhurst, I couldn't really have him staying here. I'm too old-fashioned and he always brought girls home.'

'Jessica Villiers?'

'No, he hasn't stayed here since he was a young man. I haven't heard of her.'

'The Helmsdales? Did he talk of them?'

She shook her head.

Patiently, he took her through the names of all the members of the house party. Diana

Bryce and Vera were the only names familiar to her.

Hamish then led the conversation off on to more general subjects, hoping that when he guided her back to Peter Bartlett, she might remember something to give him just one clue.

She became animated as she talked, and he guessed she was lonely. She asked him to stay to lunch, much to Miranda's obvious fury.

They were just finishing a miserable little lunch of cold quiche and limp salad when Mrs Frobisher suddenly said, 'I've just remembered. You mentioned the name of Throgmorton. Sir Humphrey Throgmorton?'

Hamish nodded.

'I've just remembered something about him. He hurt Peter's feelings very much. Peter called around to his home. Tea, I think it was. Wait a bit. It's coming back to me. Well, poor Peter broke a cup and saucer by accident, and not only did this Sir Humphrey throw a terrible scene, but he wrote to Peter's colonel-in-chief and complained. The colonel never liked Peter and this was jam to him. Peter said the old man used it as an excuse to give him the dressing down of a lifetime. Peter said Sir Humphrey was a closet homosexual and as vengeful as sin. Can you imagine anyone making such a fuss over some old china?'

'No,' said Hamish, although he privately thought that any collector would see red, given the same set of circumstances.

Mrs Frobisher looked at him almost shyly. 'I have two tickets to *Duchess Darling* – for the matinee this afternoon. I did not feel like asking someone to go with me because of Peter's death. But if you have the time . . .?'

Hamish groaned inwardly. Seeing Henry's play would remind him of Henry and that would lead to thoughts of Priscilla. He had been able to put her out of his mind while he concentrated on the case, and he did not want thoughts of her to muddle up his brain.

But the longer he spent with Mrs Frobisher, the more chance there was of her remembering more.

'I would be delighted to go,' he said. 'May I telephone someone first?'

'Of course. There's a phone over on that desk by the window. I'll go and change while you make your call.'

Hamish phoned Rory Grant at home and listened patiently while the reporter grumbled about being woken up.

'When do you start work?' asked Hamish, when he could get a word in.

'Seven o'clock this evening.'

'I might go round to the office with you. I want to look at some of the library cuttings.'

'Oh, you do, do you? They aren't cuttings any more. Everything's on computer. What's in it for me?'

'Background on these murders.'

'Okay. Do you want to come to the office, or call round here first?'

'I don't know how I'll be placed for time. If I haven't turned up at your place by six, I'll meet you at the office.'

Hamish found it hard to concentrate on the play. He was gloomily sure that Henry had somehow managed to persuade Priscilla to become re-engaged. He decided at the end of the play to go back with Mrs Frobisher and see if he could winkle any further information out of her.

The old lady was tired and leaned heavily on her cane, but there was a faint flush on her old cheeks. She had obviously enjoyed the outing.

When they got to Flood Street, Hamish said tentatively, 'I won't keep you much longer, Mrs Frobisher. I have another call to make. Could I just see some of Captain Bartlett's things?'

'I have them all in a room upstairs. The police have been through them already, of course.'

She led the way upstairs and pushed open a bedroom door. The room was, as Mrs Frobisher had said, a graveyard of hobbies. The model airplanes swung from the ceiling, a collection of rocks and fossils lay on a table, albums of stamps were piled on a chair.

'What's this?' asked Hamish, crossing the room to a little china cabinet in the corner. It contained several dainty porcelain figurines. 'Was this one of his hobbies?'

'Yes, he started collecting bits of china from the salerooms after he had been to Sir Humphrey's. Funny I should have forgotten all about Sir Humphrey until today. Peter had a sort of magpie mind. His hobbies were all other people's enthusiasms. He would take something up for a bit, throw himself into it, then he would get bored and cart the lot around to me for safekeeping.'

'Isn't it a wee bit odd,' said Hamish, studying the pieces of china, 'to think that the captain would become a collector of porcelain and yet everyone seems to think he deliberately broke a rare cup and saucer?'

'If he *did* do it deliberately,' said Mrs Frobisher loyally. 'But it's hard to explain. I do not think he had the soul of a collector, unless you call collecting other people's hobbies collecting. The china phase did not last long. What's that you've got?' she said, seeing Hamish had a ragged bunch of manuscript in his hand.

'Seem to be regimental reminiscences,' said Hamish. 'Another of his enthusiasms?'

'I suppose so,' said Mrs Frobisher. 'He scribbled from time to time.'

'Is that a fact?' said Hamish slowly. He carefully went through the room, checking any papers, reading letters, until he heard Mrs Frobisher stifle a yawn.

'I'd better be on my way,' said Hamish. He thanked her for lunch and the theatre outing and took his leave, promising to visit her the next time he was in London.

He walked back to Sloane Square and took the District Line to Blackfriars and walked along to Fleet Street. He stood for a moment at the corner of Ludgate Circus and looked up towards the great bulk of St Paul's Cathedral.

Images of the different people connected with the murder whirled around and around in his brain, facts jostled against facts, and then the kaleidoscope of bits and pieces slowly stopped revolving and settled down into a pattern.

But he had to be sure.

He set off for the *Daily Chronicle* offices at a run.

'You been drinking?' asked Rory impatiently, as he led Hamish upstairs to the reporters' desk. For Hamish was walking like a blind man, bumping into walls, his eyes fixed in an odd inward-looking stare.

'No,' said Hamish slowly. 'Look, I haff to make a call.'

'And if the night news editor comes up, how do I explain why I am letting you use the phone?'

'Tell him it is because I know who murdered

Bartlett and Vera Forbes-Grant, and I can take you with me to be in at the kill.'

'You're sure?'

Hamish rubbed the damp palms of his hands against his trousers.

'Very sure. I need one more bit of proof, and it's a long shot.'

'Go ahead and phone, and if the news editor says okay, I'll book us both on a flight.'

Hamish phoned Tommel Castle and told Jenkins to fetch Mr Chalmers.

The superintendent came on the line. 'You were right about the roach powder,' he said. 'But we're no further with solving the case.'

'This is who did it,' said Hamish.

Chalmers listened in growing amazement. 'But that's guesswork!' he exclaimed. 'Proof, laddie. Where's the proof? It's only in books that the criminal breaks down and confesses.'

'I want the name of every journalist who was there just after the first murder and who did not stay on,' said Hamish. 'I'm at the offices of the *Daily Chronicle* at the reporters' desk. I'll wait for your call.'

'You think one of *them* was an accomplice?'

'An unwitting one,' said Hamish. 'I'm making a wild guess that our criminal handed one of them a package to either keep until called for, or to take to a certain address.'

'But no journalist would be naive enough to do that?'

'Oh yes, they would, if it meant getting a bit of background and the person seemed innocent enough.'

'I've a funny feeling you're out on a limb there, Macbeth. But stay where you are until I call. It might take all night, and if it's a London journalist you're after then I'll need to ask the Yard for help.'

Rory came back looking excited. 'By God, Hamish,' he cried, 'if you can pull this one off, I'll be able to get drunk for a fortnight. What do we do now?'

'We wait,' said Hamish.

'And pray.'

Chapter Fourteen

Methought I heard a voice cry, 'Sleep no more!
Macbeth does murder sleep.

— Shakespeare

Summer lay dying outside Tommel Castle. A
chill wind blew across the moors and rattled
the windows and sent puffs of smoke from the
fire belching out into the drawing room.

They were all gathered for afternoon tea,
even Freddy Forbes-Grant, who had been
released from prison. He had stoutly main-
tained he had confessed to the murder only
because he thought his wife had committed it.
There was not enough hard evidence to hold
him. Blair swore the gloves had not been in
Freddy's room when it was first searched, and
Anderson and MacNab backed him up.
Freddy's moustache drooped, and he looked
thoroughly miserable. Mary Halburton-
Smythe poured tea with a steady hand and
tried not to think it would have been more
decent of Freddy to have mourned in his room

instead of crawling about downstairs like the skeleton at the feast.

Priscilla felt the nightmare would never end. Henry had apologized. He had said his jealousy had got the better of him and he should have realized Hamish had only a brotherly interest in her. Colonel Halburton-Smythe had taken him aside and explained everything. So much for the adult talk with her father, thought Priscilla bitterly. She was once more wearing her engagement ring. How Hamish would despise her! She felt trapped, and yet did not feel she could summon up enough courage to deal with Henry until the shadow of murder had lifted. It would be easier to cope with him in London where everything was lighter and more fickle.

The guests had been told they could leave for their respective homes on the following day, provided they did not travel anywhere else or leave the country.

'Cake?' said Mrs Halburton-Smythe brightly, holding out a plate of sliced seed cake to Pruney.

Pruney turned pale and shook her head. Everyone was drinking tea with cautious little sips, eyeing the others warily.

There came the clump of official boots and voices from the hall.

'Not again,' groaned Lady Helmsdale. 'I've made so many statements, I've given fingerprints, I've watched coppers searching my undies – I feel like shooting the lot of them.'

The door opened, and Chalmers came in. Behind him came Blair, Anderson and Mac-Nab, who took up positions round the room. Then came Hamish Macbeth, followed by what looked like a shorter, squatter version of himself – Rory Grant.

Priscilla wondered if Hamish was ill. A thin sheen of sweat filmed his face, and his eyes were hard and fixed.

'Go ahead, Macbeth,' said Chalmers quietly.

Hamish knows the identity of the murderer, thought Priscilla hysterically. He hasn't once looked at the teapot.

'It's been a difficult case,' said Hamish quietly. 'So many of you had reason to want Bartlett dead. But only one of you had the nerve, the lack of morals, and the sheer cunning to kill not only Bartlett but Mrs Forbes-Grant as well. And one of you had exceptional luck. These crimes were the work of a gifted amateur.'

He fumbled in a pocket of his tweed sports jacket and brought out a notebook and glanced down at one of the pages.

Priscilla looked around the room. Every face was tense and strained. Who did it?

'I was not absolutely sure of the identity of the killer until last night,' said Hamish.

Diana's voice rang out, high and sharp. 'You don't know at all! You haven't a clue. You're

245

watching us to see if anyone looks guilty. You've been watching too many films, just like that stupid maid.'

'No,' said Hamish. 'I know who did it. It was you . . . Henry Withering.'

There was a stunned silence.

Then Henry said in an amused voice, 'This is better than the theatre. Do go on. Why on earth should I kill Bartlett?'

'Because Captain Peter Bartlett wrote *Duchess Darling*. Not you.'

'Rubbish,' said Henry calmly. 'It's had reviews in all the papers. It's a box-office smash. He would have said something.'

'You probably changed the title. Captain Bartlett said he only read the racing papers. He knew you had a success. He'd heard that. He did not know it was his play until the night of the party I attended. Miss Smythe quoted a line from the play. Captain Bartlett looked highly amused. You were very angry and told Miss Smythe to shut up. This is how I think it happened.

'Captain Bartlett's aunt, Mrs Frobisher, said the captain had a magpie mind. He was always adopting other people's enthusiasms and hobbies. He even started collecting china after he had been to Sir Humphrey Throgmorton's.'

'What!' exclaimed Sir Humphrey, evidently more shocked by this revelation than by the identity of the murderer.

'He was living with you, Henry Withering, for a short while. You wrote plays. He decided to write one. You made out you had "written down" when you wrote *Duchess Darling*. You said you had produced something silly and trite because that was what the West End theatres wanted. I saw the play in London. I didn't think much about it until afterwards. Whoever wrote that play believed in every silly line. If I looked at it another way round and thought of the personality of Captain Bartlett, then it all made sense.'

'You're talking rot,' said Henry. No one shrank from him, not even Priscilla. It was obvious that everyone in the room thought Hamish was talking rubbish as well.

'Captain Bartlett left the play behind when he quit your flat and you found it. After a time, it dawned on you that this might just be what the public wanted. You must have enjoyed tricking them. Anyway, I think Captain Bartlett, who was a notorious gambler and sponger, confronted you with it after the party. I think he would have exposed you at the party in front of everyone – and thereby saved his life – if he had wanted to take the credit. I suggest he told you you could keep the fame so long as you passed all the money over to him. There was something about you, all the same, that made even the bold captain worried. He told me he was sure someone was out to get him. So, as insurance, he told Vera

Forbes-Grant. Miss Smythe overheard Vera saying "You can't have. I don't believe it. Not you of all people."'

Hamish turned to Freddy. 'Did your wife have any money of her own, Mr Forbes-Grant?'

'No,' said Freddy dismally. 'Not a penny. I gave her a generous allowance. But not too much. She would have left me if I had given her more. She thought I was stupid, that I didn't know she'd had an affair with Bartlett. I didn't want to lose her. I loved her.' He began to cry in a helpless, dreary way.

'Your wife may have had a soft spot for the captain,' said Hamish, 'but she loved money more than anything or anybody. She knew now what the captain had known.

'Henry was awake that night after the party, watching and waiting. Perhaps he planned to follow Bartlett when the captain went out as planned with Mr Pomfret, wait until they separated, shoot Bartlett, and throw the blame on Mr Pomfret. But he happened to see the captain going out long before the appointed time. Having rigged it to look like suicide, he returned and went to bed, confident he would never be found out. Luck had been on his side. No one else had been awake when the captain went out.

'Then Vera told him she knew Bartlett was the author of the play. I think Henry agreed to pay her while waiting his chance. As in the first murder, he waited for the right opportunity and seized it. He took a can of roach powder from the cupboard under the sink in the school kitchen, poured it into a bowl of cake mix, and then baked that batch of cakes himself. It was easily done. Everyone was milling about, beating up cake mix and putting cakes in the oven.'

'But Vera couldn't have suspected Henry,' cried Priscilla. 'She believed Freddy had done it. She was proud of him.'

'She wanted to think Freddy had done it. It made her into the *femme fatale* she'd always wanted to be. It removed any fear of Henry. Henry must have denied he murdered Bartlett. He wouldn't have wanted Vera to know that as well. She would have asked for double the money. Henry put the gloves into Freddy's room, a clumsy trick, but it paid off. Freddy thought Vera had murdered Bartlett, and so he confessed.

'I took a lot of the baking to the fair myself. But other people were going up and carrying stuff as well. Henry and Priscilla arrived with Mr and Mrs Wellington. They had boxes of cakes in the car. All Henry had to do was extract his box and put it with all the things he'd bought at the fair.

'I don't think he even needed to give Vera the cakes. He knew her passion for sweet stuff. All he had to do was put them in her room. He had nothing to do with that dummy strung up over her bed. The Chief Superintendent here already knows that was a particularly nasty trick played by Jessica Villiers and Diana Bryce.'

Jessica began to cry, but Diana looked defiantly round the room.

'You can't arrest us for a trick,' she said. 'We didn't murder Peter.'

'But Henry Withering did,' said Hamish flatly.

Henry leaned his head against the back of his chair. He appeared very relaxed and amused.

'You're guessing and you know it,' he said. 'You haven't a shred of proof.'

Hamish went out to the hall and came back in carrying a large box.

'After the supposed suicide of Bartlett had been discovered to be murder, you gave this parcel to Charles French of London Television News. You told him it was some clothes you didnae want and he was to leave it at their reception desk in London and you would pick it up when you went back south. French didn't think anything about it. You are a famous playwright. Perhaps you gave him some exclusive background.'

Hamish opened the box. 'In here,' he said, 'we have cleaning equipment from the gun room, and a pair of thin plastic gloves like the kind women wear when they're bleaching their hair. In the bathroom cabinet in your room, there was a clutter of stuff left by previous occupants, including a hairdressing product for bleaching the hair. There is also a raincoat stained with gun oil. It was clever of you. The post office would have told us if anyone from the castle had posted a parcel.' He nodded to Anderson and MacNab.

'Wait a bit,' said Colonel Halburton-Smythe. 'You cannot arrest Mr Withering. He's my daughter's fiancé!'

'All right,' said Henry. 'Now you've got that parcel, there's no point in me pretending any longer. But why couldn't it have been anyone other than you, Macbeth? To be found out by the local yokel!' He gave a harsh laugh. 'But it was the way you described it. Peter was sharing my flat. You're right about him adopting other people's enthusiasms. I was working on a play, *Animal Firm*, and he said he never went to the theatre because you couldn't see jolly plays any more. Then he said he would write one. God, how I laughed. But he had tremendous energy and could do without sleep and he worked day and night. Before he could send it to anyone, he started pursuing some girl, I forget her name. He forgot all about the play. Anyway, he wasn't paying any rent, and I told him to leave.

'I came across his stupid play one evening after *Animal Firm*, the best thing I'd ever written, had been rejected by the National Theatre. Peter's play was so awful, it was priceless. I was about to throw it away when I thought suddenly that if I polished it up a bit and changed the title, it might appeal to all the Peter Bartletts of this world who wanted something that wouldn't strain their brains. I gave it to an impresario who thought up the idea of having it expensively dressed and bringing back some of the famous lords and dames of the theatre. When it took off, I thought I'd better square Peter, but I couldn't find him. I didn't know he'd gone back to the army. When all the publicity began to appear and Peter didn't get in touch with me, I thought I was safe. The title was different and a good lot of the lines were mine – or rather, I'd polished up Peter's lines.

'When I saw him here, I felt sick. But it dawned on me very quickly he hadn't a clue I'd used his play. I didn't think he'd be likely to see it. It was ages since he'd been to the theatre. Then Pruney started quoting from it. He came to my room that night. I told him he had no way of proving it was his play, but he said he could dig up some old friends he had told at the time about it, and that he would make enough of a stink to cast doubts on the authorship. Then he said I could have the fame if he could have the money – all of it. I agreed, but I knew I'd have to kill him. Sooner or later, he'd tell someone. He was proud it had been put on and thought it a famous joke. He wouldn't have kept it secret long, not with the way he drank.' Henry fell silent. Anderson and MacNab moved towards him, but stopped as he began to speak again.

'I didn't think of shooting him. Not at first. I stayed up all night, keeping a watch on his door. I saw Vera go in and Pruney listening, but I couldn't get nearer to hear what was said. I thought if he came out to go on the prowl, I'd push him down the stairs or something like that. I nearly fell asleep, nearly *was* asleep when he came out with his shooting togs on. The rest was as you described. I put the cleaning stuff and a raincoat in that box and hid it in a bush behind one of those pillars at the gates. I knew I had to move the box because sooner or later the police would find it. Funny, if I'd just wiped my fingerprints off everything and dumped it . . . Still, I can't think of everything,' said Henry with a ghastly social smile. 'I gave the parcel to that journalist. He never thought anything odd about it. I was lucky all along. Yes, Vera blackmailed me. I had to make love to her to convince her I was a gentle, caring soul and not a murderer. I promised to pay her to keep quiet about the play. But I knew I'd have to get rid of her as well.' He turned in his chair towards Priscilla, who shrank away from him. 'No publicity is bad publicity. Isn't that right, darling?' As Anderson and MacNab came up on either side of him, he rose to his feet. 'You should see your stupid faces,' he said. And then he began to laugh. He was still laughing as they led him from the room.

The trial of Henry Withering, with all its attendant publicity, was over at last. Priscilla Halburton-Smythe, who had vague thoughts of returning to her job, stayed on at Tommel Castle instead. Winter was settling down on the Sutherland mountains.

Colonel and Mrs Halburton-Smythe had been shocked and shaken over Henry Withering's arrest. Their shock had not improved their attitude to their daughter. Fear of what might have happened to her made them treat her more like a fragile blossom than ever. They kept begging her not to return to London, to stay in Sutherland where it was 'safe' from doubtful suitors such as Henry.

It was when they said they had invited Jeremy Pomfret to dinner and made it obvious they had begun to look on him in the light of a possible son-in-law that Priscilla decided to make her escape back to London.

Jeremy, who had sworn not to stay at Tommel Castle again, had nonetheless accepted the invitation. He had enjoyed all the publicity surrounding the murder trial and seeing his picture in the newspapers, and so the cold castle had become endowed with a certain glamour in his eyes. It was small comfort to Priscilla that that glamour obviously did not extend to herself. She had not seen Hamish since the day Henry had been accused of murder. Her parents were, irrationally, furious with Hamish, blaming him obscurely for all the notoriety that had descended on their home.

Priscilla thought Hamish might have gone to Strathbane, for surely the solving of two murders would be enough to give a village constable instant promotion. She was surprised one morning to hear Jenkins complaining that Hamish Macbeth was becoming lazier and ruder every day.

All at once Priscilla wanted to see Hamish, to talk about the murder, to talk as much of it out of her brain as possible. It was a forbidden subject at Tommel Castle.

She drove down to Lochdubh, hearing her car tyres crackle over puddles of ice in the road, seeing the snowcapped mountains glittering against a pale blue sky.

The police station looked deserted and, for a moment, she thought Jenkins might have been mistaken and Hamish had left.

She made her way round the back of the station. Hamish was just climbing over the fence into his garden from the croft at the back, two empty feed pails in his hands. His red hair flamed in the sunlight and his tall, lanky figure looked safe and reassuring.

He stood for a moment watching Priscilla, and then he walked forward.

'I didn't think you were going to speak to me again,' he said.

Priscilla smiled. 'I've been upset and shocked, Hamish. But I've got over it now. I'm thinking of leaving for London next week.'

'Aye, going back to the same job?'

'No, I've lost that. It was a silly little job anyway with a miserable pay. I think I might train for something – computers or something.'

'Come into the kitchen and I'll make us some tea.'

Priscilla followed Hamish into the kitchen and sat down at the table. Towser put his head in her lap and gazed up at her soulfully.

'I thought you would have been promoted,' said Priscilla, stroking Towser's head and watching Hamish as he got the tea things out of the cupboard.

'Didn't you hear?' said Hamish. 'Poor Mr Chalmers. He died of a heart attack. Blair took the credit for everything. Didn't you read about it in the reports of the trial?'

'I wasn't called as a witness,' said Priscilla, 'and Mummy and Daddy told the servants to stop delivery of the newspapers.'

'I thought Jeremy Pomfret might have told you,' said Hamish, giving her a sidelong look.

'Jessie's been gossiping,' said Priscilla.

'Sounded to me like you were going to be Mrs Pomfret.'

'Let's not talk about Jeremy. Didn't either of

those two detectives tell anyone it was you who was responsible for solving the murders?'

'No, they have to work with Blair.'

'But Rory Grant wrote a dramatic exclusive about how you solved the murder.'

'It *was* an exclusive. The other papers, and some of them with much bigger circulations, carried Blair's version. Nobody could write anything until after the trial. Sub judice. By that time Chalmers was dead. I'm glad in a way. I like it here.'

'Yes,' said Priscilla, wondering not for the first time why Hamish's homely, cluttered police station always seemed a safer, cosier, and more welcome place than Tommel Castle.

He put a cup of tea in front of her. 'Bring it through to the living room,' he said. 'I've been making some improvements.'

Priscilla obediently walked through to the living room and then stood and looked around. There was a new carpet on the floor, a warm red shaggy carpet. The walls had been newly papered and two pretty chintz-covered armchairs were placed in front of the fire.

'This is lovely, Hamish,' said Priscilla. 'How on earth could you afford all this? I know you send every penny home.'

Hamish grinned. 'I kept a wee bit o' the grouse money back for myself.'

'The grouse money?'

'Aye, it was the morning of the murder. I found Angus, the poacher, dead-drunk down

257

at the harbour with a brace o' grouse in his back pocket. I was going to return them to your father. Well, there was the murder and all. That helicopter was standing by, and after I had taken down the pilot's statement, I remembered Captain Bartlett telling me the pilot had instructions to hand over two thousand pounds for the first brace. So I went to my car where I'd left Angus's birds and took them and handed them over.'

He beamed at her proudly.

Priscilla carefully put down her cup and got to her feet. 'A man had been shot, his chest blown away,' she said in a thin voice, 'and all you could think of, you great moocher, was how to turn it to your advantage!'

She turned and ran from the house.

Hamish stood for a moment, staring at the spot where she had been.

Then he sprinted out of the room, out of the house and into the garden.

Priscilla was standing by her car, leaning her head on the roof. Her shoulders were shaking.

He came cautiously up behind her. 'Dinnae take it so hard,' he pleaded. 'It iss not me who's the murderer.'

She turned round and buried her face on his shoulder.

'Priscilla,' said Hamish suspiciously, 'I have a feeling you're laughing.' He tilted up her head.

'Oh, Hamish,' giggled Priscilla, 'you are the most shocking man I know.'

Hamish rolled his eyes. 'Do you hear?' he cried to a passing seagull. 'Here's her that gets engaged tae criminals telling the force of law and order in Lochdubh that he's shocking. Come along then, Priscilla, and I'll get us something to eat.'

'What? Grouse?' demanded Priscilla, still giggling.

'Aye, I just might hae a wee bit.'

With a companionable arm about her shoulders, he led her towards the police station, pushed her gently inside, followed her in, and closed the door firmly behind them on the cold outside world.

If you enjoyed *Death of a Cad*, read on for the first chapter of the next book in the *Hamish Macbeth* series . . .

Death of an Outsider

Chapter One

See, the happy moron,
He doesn't give a damn,
I wish I were a moron,
My God! Perhaps I am!
– Anonymous

Constable Hamish Macbeth sat in the small
country bus that was bearing him away from
Lochdubh – away from the west coast of
Sutherland, away from his police-station
home. His dog, Towser, a great yellowish
mongrel, put a large paw on his knee, but the
policeman did not notice. The dog sighed and
heaved itself up on to the seat beside him
and joined his master in staring out of the
window.

The bus driver was new to the job. 'Nae
dugs on the seats,' he growled over his shoulder, determined not to be intimidated by
Hamish's uniform. But the constable gave
him a look of such vacant stupidity that the
driver, a Lowland Scot who considered all

Highlanders inbred, decided it was useless to pursue the matter.

Misery *did* make Hamish Macbeth look dull-witted. It seemed as if only a short time ago he had been happy and comfortable in his own police station in Lochdubh, and then orders had come that he was to relieve Sergeant MacGregor at Cnothan, a crofting town in the centre of Sutherland. In vain had he invented a crime wave in Lochdubh. He was told that protecting the occasional battered wife and arresting a drunk once every two months did not amount to a crime wave. He was to lock up the police station and go by bus, for Sergeant MacGregor wished his stand-in to keep his car in running order.

Hamish hated change almost as much as he hated work. He had the tenancy of some croft land next to the police station at Lochdubh, where he kept a small herd of sheep, now being looked after by a neighbour. He earned quite good money on the side from his small farming, his poaching, and the prize money he won for hill running at the Highland Games in the summer. All that he could save went to his mother and father and brothers and sisters over in Cromarty. He did not anticipate any easy pickings in Cnothan.

Crofters, or hill farmers, always need another job because usually the croft or small-holding is too small a farm to supply a liveli-hood. So crofters are also postmen, forestry workers, shopkeepers, and, in the rare case of Hamish Macbeth, policemen.

It was the end of January, and the north of Scotland was still in the grip of almost perpetual night. The sun rose shortly after nine in the morning, where it sulked along the horizon for a few hours before disappearing around two in the afternoon. The fields were brown and scraggly, the heather moors, dismal rain-sodden wastes, and ghostly wreaths of mist hung on the sides of the tall mountains.

There were only a few passengers on the bus. The Currie sisters, Jessie and Nessie, two spinster residents of Lochdubh, were talking in high shrill voices. 'Amn't I just telling you, Nessie?' came the voice of Jessie. 'I went over to the Royal Society for the Prevention of Cruelty to Animals at Strathbane last week and I says to the mannie, "I want a humane trap to catch the ferret that has been savaging our ducks." He gives me the trap, and he says, "You take this here humane trap, and you humanely catch your ferret, and then, if you want my advice, you will humanely club the wee bastard to death." Sich a going-on! And him supposed to be against cruelty. I have written to our Member of Parliament to complain most strongly.'

'You told me a hundred times,' grumbled Nessie. 'Maybe he was right. For all you caught in that humane trap was the minister's cat. Why don't you tell Mr Macbeth about it?'

'Him!' screeched Jessie. 'That constable is a poacher and it was probably his ferret.'

The bus jerked to a halt and the sisters alighted, still quarrelling.

Three months in Cnothan, thought Hamish, absent-mindedly scratching Towser behind the ears. They say Lochdubh is quiet, but nothing ever happens in Cnothan, and nothing ever will. Did I not have the two murders in Lochdubh?

He thought of the murder that had taken place last summer and how it appeared to have brought him closer to the love of his life, Priscilla Halburton-Smythe. But Priscilla, the daughter of a local landowner, had then left, just before Christmas, to go to London to find work. She never stayed away for very long. She might even be heading north now, and would return to Lochdubh to find him gone.

'And she will not be caring one little bit!' said Hamish suddenly and loudly. The bus driver bent over the wheel and congratulated himself on his decision to leave this crazy copper alone.

Hamish knew Cnothan and thought it must be the dullest place in the world. Although designated a town, it was about the size of a tiny English village. He remembered the inhabitants as being a close, secretive, religious bunch who considered anyone from outside an interloper.

At last, he was the only passenger left on the bus. The bus lurched and screeched around hairpin bends, finally racing out of the shadow of the tall pillared mountains to plunge down into the valley where Cnothan stood, in the middle of Sutherland.

Hamish climbed down stiffly and collected his belongings, which were packed into a haversack and an old leather suitcase. The bus departed with a roar and Hamish pushed his peaked hat back on his fiery hair and looked about him.

'High noon in Cnothan,' he muttered.

It was the lunch hour, which meant all the shops were closed and the main street was deserted. A savage wind screamed down it. Not even a piece of scrap paper was borne on the wind. The town had a scrubbed, grey, antiseptic look.

Cnothan stood on the edge of an artificial loch caused by one of the ugliest hydroelectric dams Hamish had ever seen. What you saw was what you got. There were no quaint lanes or turnings. One straight main street led down to the loch. There were four grocer's shops, which all sold pretty much the same sort of goods, a hardware, a garage, a craft shop, a hotel, a fish-and-chip shop, a butcher's, a pub, and an enormous church. The government-subsidized housing was tucked away on the other side of the loch, segregated from Cnothan's privately owned houses, which were all very small and drab and looked remarkably like the government ones.

The town was so barren, so empty, it reminded Hamish of scenes in a science-fiction movie he had once seen.

And yet he was aware of eyes watching him, eyes hidden behind the neatly drawn lace curtains.

He opened the garden gate of the bungalow nearest him, called Green Pastures, and went up and rang the brass ship's bell that hung outside the door. Silence. A plaster gnome stared at him from the garden and the wind moaned drearily.

A mail-order magazine protruded from the rubbish bin beside the door. Hamish twisted his head and read the name on it. Mrs A. MacNeill. At last he heard footsteps approaching. The door was opened a few inches on a chain and a woman's face peered through the crack, one of those sallow Spanish types of faces you find in the Highlands of Scotland.

'What is it?' she demanded.

Now Hamish knew in that instant that the woman knew exactly who he was. Her manner was too calm. For in a relatively crime-free area, the arrival of a policeman on the doorstep usually creates terror because it means news of a death or accident.

'I am Constable Macbeth,' said Hamish pleasantly, 'come to replace Mr MacGregor who is going on holiday. Where is the police station?'

'I dinnae ken,' said the woman. 'Maybe it's up the hill.'

'At the top of the main street?' asked Hamish. He knew the woman knew perfectly well where the police station was, but Hamish was an incomer, and in Cnothan, you never told incomers anything if you could help it.

'It could be, but why don't you ask someone else?' said the face at the door.

Hamish leaned against the door jamb and studied the sky. 'Aye, it iss blowing up,' he said in his soft Highland voice, which became more sibilant when he was angry or upset. 'Now, Mr MacGregor, he will be going to Florida to visit his brother, Roy. It will be hot there this time of year.'

'Aye, it will,' said the woman.

'And I call to mind he has the sister in Canada.'

The chain dropped and the door opened another few inches. 'That's Bessie,' said the woman. 'Her that is in Alberta.'

'True, true,' agreed Hamish. 'And you are Mrs MacNeill?'

'Now, how did you ken that?' asked Mrs MacNeill, opening the door wide.

'Oh, hass not everyone heard of Mrs Mac-Neill,' said Hamish. 'That's why I called. People are not often anxious to give directions, but I said to myself, that Mrs MacNeill, being a cosmopolitan sort of lady, would help if she could.'

Mrs MacNeill simpered awfully. 'You are asking about the police station. Yes, as I was saying, it is right at the top of the main street on the left. They are packed and ready to leave.'

'Thank you.' Hamish touched his cap and strolled off. 'Cantankerous auld bitch,' he muttered to Towser, 'but there was no point in asking anyone else, for I suppose they'll all be the same.'

At the top of the main street was a long, low, grey bungalow with the blue police lamp over an extension to the side. A small angry police sergeant was striding up and down outside.

'What kept ye?' he snapped. And then, before Hamish could open his mouth, he went on, 'Come in. Come in. But leave that dog outside. There's an old kennel at the back. It can sleep there. No dogs in the house.'

Hamish told Towser to stay and followed the sergeant into the house. The sergeant led the way through to the extension. 'Here's the desk, and don't you mess up my filing system. And there's the keys to the cell. You'll have trouble wi' Sandy Carmichael of a Saturday. Gets the horrors something dreadful.'

'If a man has the DTs, isn't it better to get him to the hospital?' asked Hamish mildly.

'Waste o' public money. Jist strap him down on the bunk and let him rave away until morning. Come ben and meet the wife.'

Hamish loped behind the bustling policeman. 'She's in the lounge,' said Sergeant MacGregor. Mrs MacGregor rose to meet them. She was a thin, wispy woman with pale

270

eyes and enormous red hands. Hamish's pleasantries were cut short.

'I like to keep the place nice,' said Mrs Mac-Gregor. 'I don't want to come back from Florida and find the place like a tip.'

Hamish stood with his cap under his arm, his hazel eyes growing blanker by the minute. The living-room in which he stood, which had been exalted to a lounge by the MacGregors, was a long, low room with pink ruched curtains at the windows. A salmon-coloured three-piece suite, which looked as if it had been delivered that day, stared back at him in all its nylon velveteen overstuffedness. The walls were embellished with highly coloured religious pictures. A blond and blue-eyed Jesus suffered the little children to come unto him, all of them dressed in thirties school clothes and all of them remarkably Anglo-Saxon-looking. A carpet of one of the more violent Scottish tartans screamed from the floor. There was a glass coffee-table on wrought iron legs in front of the sofa, and a glass-and-wrought iron bar stood in one corner, with glass shelves behind it lit with pink fluorescent strip lighting and containing, it seemed, every funny-looking bottle ever invented. An electric heater with fake logs stood in the fireplace. In the recesses of the room were glass shelves containing a startling variety of china ornaments: acid-green jugs in the shape of fish, little girls in pastel dresses holding up their skirts, bowls of china fruit, dogs and cats with Disney smiles on their highly glazed faces, and rows of miniature spun-glass objects, of the type of spun glass you see at fairgrounds. On a side table lay a large Victorian Bible, open at a page where there was a steel engraving of an epicene angel with scaly wings throwing very small anguished people in loincloths down into a fiery pit.

Mrs MacGregor then led him from one frilly overfurnished bedroom to another. The bungalow boasted five.

'Where's the kitchen?' asked Hamish, finding his voice.

She trotted on her high heels in front of him, head down, as if charging. 'In here,' she said. Hamish stifled a sigh of relief. The kitchen was functional and had every labour-saving device imaginable. The floor was tiled, and there was a good-sized table. He decided to shut off that terrible lounge for the duration of his stay.

'Have you got television?' he asked.

Mrs MacGregor looked up at the tall, gangling policeman with the fiery-red hair and hazel eyes. 'No, we don't believe in it,' she said sharply, as if debating the existence of little green men on Mars.

'I see you have the central heating,' remarked Hamish.

'Yes, but we have double glazing on the windows, so you'll find you hardly need it. It's on a timer. Two hours in the morning and two in the evening, and that's enough for anyone.'

'Well, if I could chust haff a word with your good man . . .' began Hamish, looking around for the police sergeant, who had disappeared during the tour of the house.

'There's no time, no time,' she said, seizing a bulging handbag from the kitchen counter. 'Geordie's waiting with the taxi.'

Hamish looked at her in amazement. He wanted to ask MacGregor about duties, about where the keys to the car were kept, about how far his beat extended, about the villains of the parish. But he was sure the MacGregors were cursed with what he had rapidly come to think of as Cnothanitis: Don't tell anyone anything.

He followed her out to the taxi. 'So you'll be away three months, then?' said Hamish, leaning on MacGregor's side of the taxi. The sergeant stared straight ahead. 'If you'd get out of the road, Constable,' he said, 'we might be able to get to the train on time.'

'Wait a bit,' said Hamish. 'Where are the keys to your car?'

'In it,' snapped MacGregor. He nodded to the taxi driver and the cab moved off.

'Good riddance,' grumbled Hamish. He jerked his head to Towser, who followed him into the kitchen. Hamish took the central heating off the timing regulator and turned up the thermostat as high as it would go and started to examine the contents of the kitchen cupboards to see if there was any coffee. But the cupboards were bare; not even a packet of salt.

'You know, Towser,' said Hamish Macbeth, 'I hope they get hijacked to Cuba.'

He went through to the office and examined the files in a tall filing cabinet in the corner. It was full of sheep-dip papers and little else. Not dipping one's sheep seemed to be considered the major criminal offence in Cnothan. There came a crashing and rattling from the kitchen. He ran through. Towser had his large head in one of the bottom cupboards, which Hamish had left open, and was rummaging through the pots and pans.

'Get out of it, you daft animal,' said Hamish. 'I'll just away to the shops and see if I can get us some food.' He searched until he found a bowl and filled it with water for the dog. Then he ambled out of the house and down the main street. The lunch hour was over and the shops were open again. People were standing in little knots, gossiping, and as he passed, they stopped talking and stared at him with curious and unfriendly eyes.

He bought two bags of groceries and then made his way down to the garage, which also sold household goods. He asked if he could rent a television set and was curtly told by a small man whose face was set in lines of perpetual outrage that no, he could not. To the shopkeeper's irritation, Hamish did not go away, but kept repeating his question in a half-witted sort of manner, looking around the other customers as he did so.

A small, thin, birdlike woman with sharp features came up to him. 'You will be Mr MacGregor's replacement,' she said briskly. 'I am Mrs Struthers, the minister's wife. Can we expect to see you at church on Sunday?'

'Oh, yes,' said Hamish amiably. 'My name's Macbeth. I am a member of the Free Church myself.' Hamish had taken careful note of the denomination of Cnothan's main church. He was not a member of the Free Church, or, indeed, of any other church.

'Well, that's splendid!' cried Mrs Struthers. 'Now, I heard you asking about a telly. We have a black-and-white one we are going to raffle at Easter. I could lend you that.'

'Very kind of you,' said Hamish, smiling down at her. That smile changed his whole face. It was a smile of singular sweetness.

In no time at all, Hamish was resting his boots on a footstool in the manse and being plied with tea and scones.

'I am thinking, Mrs Struthers,' said Hamish, 'that it will be a wee bit difficult for me here. They never did like incomers in Cnothan.'

'Well . . .' said Mrs Struthers cautiously, going to the window to make sure there was no sign of her husband returning from his rounds, her husband having preached about the iniquities of gossip the previous Sunday, 'people here are very nice when you get to know them. All it takes is a few years.'

'I haven't got the time,' said Hamish. 'I'm only here for three months.'

'They'll come around quicker,' she said, 'because they're all united against a really nasty incomer.' She looked around and her voice dropped to a whisper. 'An Englishman.'

'Oh dear,' said Hamish encouragingly. 'They do not like the English?'

'It's not that,' said the minister's wife. 'It's just he's such a know-all. It's a crofting community round here. They don't like being told how to run things, particularly by an outsider, but Mr Mainwaring, that's his name, *will* tell them what they are doing wrong. Not in a nasty way, mind. But as if he's laughing at them. His poor wife. He won't even leave her to run the house, but supervises her cooking. He even *chooses her clothes* for her!'

'The fiend!' cried Hamish, registering extreme shock, very gratifying to the minister's wife, who had not had such an appreciative audience in years.

'Have another scone, Constable. Yes, she is a member of the Women's Rural Institute and gave us a very good lecture on how to dry and arrange flowers. Most stimulating. She was doing very well, but he walked in at the question time and started grilling her – his own wife!'

'Fancy!'

'Yes. And she turned as red as fire and began to stammer. Wicked it was. And . . .'

The sound of a car crunching on the gravel outside made Mrs Struthers turn as red as fire

276

herself. 'I had better go,' said Hamish, not wishing to waste time talking to the minister.

But as he rose to his feet, Mr Struthers, the minister, came in. He had a pale face and pale-blue eyes and a thin mouth. His tow-coloured hair was carefully sleeked down. Mrs Struthers, rather flustered, made the introductions. 'I trust you have not been gossiping,' said the minister severely.

'On the contrary,' said Hamish, 'your good lady has just been encouraging me to visit the kirk on the Sabbath. She was telling me all about your powerful sermons.'

He shook hands with the minister, collected the small television set, and said goodbye. The minister's wife went to the window and watched the tall figure of the constable as he walked away with a rather dreamy smile on her face. 'Such a fine man,' she murmured.

Hamish ambled up the main street, comfortably full of tea and home-made scones and jam. At the top, opposite the police station, he noticed an old cottage, set a little back from the road, with a sign outside which said, PAINTINGS FOR SALE.

There was what appeared to be a teenage girl digging the garden. As if aware she was being watched, she turned around, saw Hamish, and came up to the garden gate. Her figure was as trim and youthful as a girl's, but Hamish judged her to be about the same age as himself – in her thirties. She had an elfin face, a wide smile, and a mop of black curls.

'Jenny Lovelace,' she said, holding out a small, earthy hand.

'Hamish Macbeth,' said Hamish, smiling down at her. 'Is that an American accent?'

'No, Canadian.'

'And what are you doing in the wilds of Sutherland, Miss Lovelace?' asked Hamish, putting down the television set and two grocery bags on the ground and shaking her hand before leaning comfortably on the gate.

'I wanted peace and quiet. I came over on a holiday and stayed. I've been here four years.'

'And do you like it? I gather they don't like incomers here.'

'Oh, I get along all right. I like being alone.'

'I get the idea life has been easier for the incomers since a certain Mr Mainwaring arrived. He sounds like a right pain in the neck.'

Jenny's face hardened. 'Mr Mainwaring is about the only civilized person in the whole of this place,' she said sharply.

'I always go and put my big foot in it,' said Hamish sadly. 'It comes from not being in the way of talking to pretty girls. My mind gets all thumbs.'

Jenny giggled. 'Your mind doesn't have thumbs,' she said. 'Gracious! What's that terrible howling coming from the police station?'

'It's my dog, Towser. He wants his food, and when he wants his food, he screams for it. I'd best be on my way.'

'Drop round for a coffee,' said Jenny, turning away, as Hamish stooped to pick up his belongings.

'When?' Hamish called after her.

'Any time you like.'

'I'll drop by the morn,' called Hamish, feeling suddenly happy.

Towser's howling stopped when he saw his master. He lay on the kitchen floor and stared at Hamish with sorrowful eyes. 'I've got some liver for ye,' grumbled Hamish, pouring oil in a pan. 'See, low cholesterol oil, good for your fat heart.' The doorbell on the police-station extension sounded shrilly. Hamish made a move to answer it. Towser started to howl again.

Hamish ran and wrenched open the door. A middle-aged man stood on the step. He was tall, well-built, and had a large round head and neat prim features, small round eyes, a button of a nose, and a small primped mouth. Although he must have been nearly sixty, he had a thick head of brown hair, worn long so that it curled over his collar. He was wearing a waxed coat with a corduroy collar, gabardine breeches, lovat stockings, and brogues – and a red pullover. English, thought Hamish. They aye love thae red pullovers.

'Come in and I'll be with you in a minute,' gabbled Hamish as Towser's howling rose to a crescendo. Hamish darted back to the kitchen and put the liver in the frying pan. When it was ready, he cut it up into small pieces, arranged it on a dish, and put it in front of the dog.

'So we've lost one fool of a policeman to find another,' said a sarcastic upper-class-accented voice from the doorway of the kitchen. 'Let me tell you, Constable, that I am going to write to your superiors and say that feeding good butcher's meat to a spoilt mongrel takes precedence in what's left of your mind over solving crime.'

'Sit yerself down, Mr Mainwaring,' said Hamish, 'and I'll attend to you. I havenae had time to draw breath since I arrived.'

'How do you know my name?'

'Your reputation goes before you,' said Hamish. 'Now, we can stand here exchanging insults or we can get down to business. What's the crime?'

William Mainwaring drew out a kitchen chair and sat down and looked up at the tall policeman. He took out a pipe and lit it with precise, fussy movements. Hamish waited patiently.

'You ask me what the crime is?' said Mainwaring finally. 'Well, I'll tell you in one word:

'Witchcraft.'